# BEST EROTIC ROMANCE OF THE YEAR

VOLUME ONE

# BEST EROTIC ROMANCE OF THE YEAR

## VOLUME ONE

*Edited by*
KRISTINA WRIGHT

*Foreword by*
TIFFANY REISZ

Published in the United States by Cleis Press, an imprint of Start Midnight, LLC, 101 Hudson Street, 37th Floor, Suite 3705, Jersey City, NJ 07302.

Printed in the United States.
Cover design: Scott Idleman/Blink
Text design: Frank Wiedemann

First Edition.
10 9 8 7 6 5 4 3 2 1

Trade paper ISBN: 978-1-62778-113-8
E-book ISBN: 978-1-62778-114-5

*For Jay,*
*always*

# CONTENTS

# FOREWORD

Tiffany Reisz

"I'm madly in love with someone. I hope he never ever touches me," said no one ever.

Erotic romance—it's a strange term. Almost redundant. Eros, from which the word *erotic* comes, was the original god of love in ancient Greek mythology. From the very dawn of human story-telling, we were associating eros with love. Eros and romance were one and the same then and still are today. Even in the Bible sex and love are intimately intertwined. The Song of Solomon celebrates romantic and sexual love with lyrics like "Let him kiss me with the kisses of his mouth for your love is sweeter than wine." And even in the Garden of Eden, God gave Adam and Eve the command to be fruitful and multiply. God told them to fuck, and they fucked (and then they fucked up).

When we speak of erotic romance, the book genre, we're talking about a specific type of romance novel—a romance novel wherein the sexual relationship drives the story forward. The couple (or trio in a ménage) fall into bed early in the story and the dramatic tension is romantic—will they fall in love and stay together? This stands in contrast to more traditional romances where the love happens early and the dramatic tension is sexual—will they ever get in bed? And if so, will they stay there? Please and spank you?

In an erotic romance the reader is made two promises by the writer—the characters will fall in love and be together at the end of the book. And they'll fuck. Hard and often and with every little detail of said fucking supplied to the reader. If there's no fucking, it's not erotic. If there's no happy ending, it's not a romance. If it's called an erotic romance you get the best of romance and the best of erotica in one book.

The most important sex organ is the brain. Sex starts in the brain. We desire our partner, fantasize about him or her, plan a seduction, dream a rendezvous… Or, like me and like the authors of the stories in this volume of erotic romance, we write. We write passionate love and lust stories that explore the endless varieties of ways people fall in love, make love, fight for love and fuck when the fighting is over and everybody's won.

The writers of erotic romances are true believers in the power of love. But love itself isn't enough to sustain a relationship. We're adult women (and a few men), all of us who write it, and we love sex, love having sex, love reading about sex and love writing sex. Studies show that people who have regular sex tend to be physically healthier, have lower stress levels, sleep better, and maintain lower blood pressure. Sex is one of life's great comforts—no calories, no unpleasant side effects and you can have it alone or with a partner.

Or you can have it by reading this anthology of erotic romance stories. So if anyone asks what you're doing tonight, tell them you're going to bed with eighteen women.

# INTRODUCTION: ONLY THE BEST

As I write this, I've just seen the book cover for the Turkish translation of my cross-genre relationship guide *Bedded Bliss: A Couple's Guide to Lust Ever After*. The new title, *Vanilya Kokusu*, translates as "Vanilla Scent." Which didn't seem to have much to do with the book, until I saw a (translated) description that references my introduction talking about "vanilla" sex and how vanilla gets a bad rap when, in fact, it's not only the most popular flavor of ice cream, it's the most popular kind of sex. And, as my friend Sarah (a Naval officer who is currently stationed in Turkey) reminded me, the scent of vanilla is a combination of "intoxication and comfort"—you can't just take one sniff, it's addictive. And so, as I sit in my backyard in Virginia, I'm delighted to know that readers in Turkey are enjoying the stories and advice in a relationship guide I wrote and edited.

So, what does that have to do with *Best Erotic Romance of the Year*? Here's the thing, dear reader: I write and edit these books, never thinking too much beyond my own backyard.

Sure, I know you're out there, buying my books and reading the stories I've selected, and I keep you in mind at all times—I want you to fall in love with the stories I write and choose just as I have fallen in love with them. But I think I sometimes forget how far these books travel and how many people, in all sorts of different places, will read this book. Knowing my words have been translated into French, German, and yes, even Turkish, is a reminder of the most important lesson of love: it is universal. We all want it, need it, *crave* it. Not just me, here in my wooded yard in sunny Virginia, but men and women everywhere.

And so, as I put the finishing touches on this collection, I'm reminded of you, the reader. Whether you live down the street or across the country or on the other side of the world. You are why I write, why I curate anthologies, why I believe in love and passion as a delicious—and universal—combination. We may never enjoy a meal together or share a cup of coffee or even speak the same language, but we both believe in desire and we both want to read a good story that reminds us that true, passionate love lasts forever.

And so I present to you the best of the best, from my backyard to yours, wherever in the world you may be. Happy reading!

Kristina Wright
Chesapeake, Virginia

# SIREN'S SONG

Renee Luke

Taking a breath and closing her eyes, Melody Davis gripped the mic with both hands. A mist of sweat dampened her palms as they wrapped around the welcome coolness of metal. Her heart thumped hard in her chest. Her hands trembled. It wasn't nervousness that caused the shake, but excitement. An uncoiling of energy that started as a light flutter in her belly, but poured though her system like a shot of whiskey. Energy mingled with relief.

With her lids closed and her lashes settled on her cheeks, she fell into the rhythm, allowed it to consume her. The dance of ivory keys mimicked her pulse. The brass sax's siren song spoke to her soul.

Breathing deeply, she tried to steady herself, to find her center and peace. She waited all week—every week—for Friday nights when she got to get on stage at Margie's little hole-in-the-wall bar and sing. Margie's wasn't on Bourbon Street. Hell, it wasn't even in the French Quarter.

But Bourbon Street didn't matter. The French Quarter didn't matter. The only thing that mattered was that she had the opportunity to get on stage and sing. She didn't sing because she wanted to, but because she had to. She needed to. Needed to sing like she needed to breathe.

The rat-a-tat clash of hi-hats joined the piano. Melody swallowed. Her moment was coming. Exhilaration sped through body, every part of her throbbing with awareness. Heat prickled across her skin. Her nipples puckered. Melody smiled, intoxicated by the feeling. A musical seduction.

The bass drum dropped. She felt the vibration as much as she heard it. Holding onto the mic, the stand her dance partner, her hips began to sway, the tempo controlling her. She fell into the beat, opened her mouth and began to sing. The lyrics came naturally. She lived them. She breathed them.

Her body operated on muscle memory as she finished one song, telling the story of love and longing and heartache, and drifted easily into another. The measure changed. The words were different. The way singing made her feel remained a constant, and addicting. Her body responded to each cadence change, worked in unison with the band. She was no longer singing along, but her voice an instrument.

Smiling as the music finally began to fade out, Melody knew they'd been playing for hours, her throat getting that tickle of dryness that always signified the end of her time. She seemed to float away as she sang, to go to a place of happiness where she felt but didn't think. Time held no significance. The music stopped but her pulse still hummed in her ears. Awareness still pirouetted across her skin. Motionless, her breaths coming in short, shallow pants, she struggled to regain composure and put her emotions in check. She was always so raw, her soul exposed, at the end of a set.

It wasn't until when she heard the band members moving around the stage and putting away their instruments that Melody let out a breath and opened her eyes. Most of the lights had been cut off, except the neon signs illuminating the bar and exit. The cigarette smoke lingered, but was beginning to fade. Margie's was dim. And empty.

Melody scanned the bar as her eyes adjusted. That's when she saw him. Tyrrell Jones: damn, that man was delicious. He sat lounging in darkness in the back, tilted on a small wooden chair that seemed too little for his muscular frame. Tyrrell had been tending bar at Margie's as long as she'd been singing there.

Tyrrell Jones was one of the reasons she sang with her eyes closed. Looking at him was too distracting. Singing was an aphrodisiac to her, her body responsive and on fire. Her skin begged to be touched, her pussy purred to be petted. Tension coiled tightly while she sang, her senses heightened. Singing made her feel alive. Tyrrell made her feel desire.

*Breathe*, she reminded herself as air burned in her lungs, her focus on the man in the shadows. Even with the lack of light, she could make out the mixture of emotions etched on his face. The slight smile on his lickable lips was at odds with the brooding in his dark eyes.

Her heart paused and then skipped into a quick beat. Their gaze caught and held. She was shaking again so she tightened her hands around the mic and held on.

"Goodnight, Miss Melody," Josh, her piano player said. "You did great tonight."

The other band members echoed his words as they shuffled around gathering their things.

Melody smiled. "Thank you, guys. You guys were amazing." She cleared her throat. "Have a good night." She spoke to the band, but her gaze never left the man seated at the back of the room. Behind her, she could hear more good-byes as they went out the back and parted ways.

Taking a breath, Melody released the mic and stepped away. She tore her gaze from him and glanced around the room. "I guess I chased everyone out." She laughed.

"Nah, Melody, you're the reason they come here." There was a pause. "It's late, is all."

Lawd, she loved his voice. The timbre so low and rich. He hadn't moved, but she could feel his stare on her skin and his voice felt like he'd caressed her with velvet. She strolled across the stage, lifted the hem of her dress, and then stepped down the three wooden stairs along the side. "I'm sorry to have played over, Tyrrell."

Her stilettos tapped the floor as she walked across the room. As she approached she noticed a glass mug of beer on the round table to Tyrrell's left. Dew clung to the glass, and she could tell it'd been sitting there untouched for a while because the froth had died away. Even if it was a little flat, she was tempted to take a drink to ease the tightness in her throat. She glanced at him. "Sometimes it feels so good, I don't want to stop." Heat splashed her cheeks, realization of how her words could be taken quickly dawning.

A growl escaped from the back of his throat, but the sound became a chuckle and he pushed to his feet. "It's no trouble." He cleared his throat as he glanced in the direction of his drink. "Got distracted by listening to you sing. Just gotta finish up a few things before close."

He stood before her. Towering over her. All muscle and swagger. Loose jeans clung to his body. A dark-blue MARGIE'S BAR T-shirt showed every contour of his wide shoulders and chiseled abs. Melody swallowed. She balled her hands into fists to keep from reaching for him, her palms itching to replace the cotton, to smooth over his perfect milk-chocolate skin.

It was past four in the morning but she was wide-awake. Even if she left, it would be hours before she'd come down from her performance high. Hours of tossing and turning and yearning before she'd find sleep. She gulped. "It's my fault. So I'll help you."

Tyrrell tightened his jaw. There were a few things that were Melody's fault tonight and not finishing closing was the least concerning of them all. Hell no, closing the bar was shit compared to his rocked-up dick, swollen and aching trapped behind his boxers and jeans. Would Melody help him with that?

Did she know that she made innocent look sexy as fuck, standing there in a little piece of pale blue satin that looked more like a nightie than a dress? Her wide eyes were the amber color of his beer, only more intoxicating. Her lips were lush, naturally pink, and accentuated words in a way that when she spoke he couldn't help but think they were meant to be wrapped around his dick.

"Don't worry about it, Melody." Reaching back, he placed his hand on the back of his head and rubbed out a knot of tension forming at the base of his neck. He didn't want Melody to leave, but didn't trust himself to not act on his desire for her if she didn't. He cleared his throat. "Not your fault, and you've already had a long night." Over the years, he'd made a point to not be alone with her. Until tonight. He hadn't meant to be caught watching.

And now she was watching him, her gaze resolute and inquisitive. Her perfect lush mouth opened and closed twice like she was about to say something. But didn't. No words came out, but his dick throbbed like she'd issued an invitation. And damn he wanted to accept. Claim her mouth with his. Kiss her until she was pliable and out of breath. One tug on the thin satin straps and she'd be standing naked in nothing but heels. Blood rushed to his erection. Lust made it hard to think.

"What do I have to do?" she asked.

*Let me fuck you senseless…* Tyrrell shook his head. What she had to do was wrap those legs around his waist and let him in.

"Nothing."

Something defiant flashed in her eyes and a smile dashed across her full lips. "Tyrrell," she whispered as she reached forward and touched his arm, "I'm helping, so tell me what to do."

The contact was light, but her skin soft and warm. She touched his arm, but his dick reacted like she'd stroked it from base to head, pulsing heavy against his gut. He wanted to grab her up, toss her over his shoulder and carry her off someplace to devour her fully. Instead, he stepped away.

Picking up his tepid, flat beer, he drained the liquid, but it didn't do much to soothe the tightness in his throat, the desire burning in his gut or the lust rocking up his dick. He cleared his throat. "Wash and sanitize the last of the glasses," he replied, lifting the empty beer mug as an example. "Wipe down the bar and mop."

"Perfect." She took the mug from him.

"Perfect?"

She nodded. "I'll do the glasses. Give me a quick lesson." Slanted her head, she pursed her lips.

Tyrrell laughed. She wasn't taking no as an answer. He studied her face for a moment. She could ask him anything. He wouldn't say no, either. "Okay, Melody. Runs pretty much like a dishwasher." He stepped aside and held his arm out to direct her to the kitchen.

She glanced back at him as she walked by. "You're actually doing me a favor, Tyrrell, by allowing me to help."

"Oh yeah, how's that?"

"I'm always so wound up after performing..."

They arrived at the double aluminum sink and he reached over and turned on the faucet, filling the first sink with suds and hot water.

"So this will give me a chance to unwind." Swirling her fingers in the soap bubbles she became quiet, but her eyes stormed something secretive and erotic.

Tyrrell stood captivated by her, her words low and calming, but her gaze tempestuous. His pulse throbbed. Air burned in his chest, held in his lungs while he waited for her to continue.

For a moment, silence draped over them, but it was a comfortable quiet and it gave him a moment to just appreciate her nearness. He'd stayed working at Margie's because of her. He could've made a lot more money leaving the Seventeenth Ward and tending bar in the French Quarter, but that would mean not seeing her sing every Friday night. She was worth every penny he lost.

His heart ached. He'd first fallen for her the day they met. She sang to get the gig rather than using her family name, never once mentioning her great-uncle Miles. She stood on her own strength and talent. He dug that shit and had been instantly attracted like a moth to light. Melody Davis was pure light and he was consumed by his need for her.

Tyrrell gulped, clenching his hands at his sides to keep from reaching for her. He'd spent years fantasizing about this. About being alone with her. One little *yes* indication from Melody and he'd make every fantasy a reality.

She flicked bubbles at him. "What's next?"

He shook his head. *What's next? Sex. Now I get my dick wet and you scream my name*. Damn, he was about to burst. Clearing his throat, he replied. "A quick wash here, rinse here."

He indicated the second sink and then opened the steam sanitizer. "Then load the baskets and press start."

"Simple enough."

"For sure."

She giggled, the sound musical in his ears. "So stop babysitting me and go do your own chores." She lifted her chin as she smiled, her eyes shimmering. "It'll be almost dawn when we get outta here. Maybe we…" her voice trailed off and she worried her bottom lip between her teeth, her fiery gaze holding his. "I'll get started." She turned away and started filling the soap sink with drink glasses.

Tyrrell watched her for a moment. The damn back of the dress revealed more skin that the front. Her shoulders were bare; the creaminess of her skin made his mouth water. The material plunged low on her back. Where the satin gapped, he could see the shadow of her thin waist and the plump roundness of her ass. Perfect cheeks to hold on to when he was grinding into her.

Tearing himself away, he adjusted his jeans to make room for his hard-on. He left her standing by the sink and went to fill the mop bucket. If he didn't force himself to get to work she'd finish the dishes and he'd still be lingering there like a damn fool, drooling over a piece of forbidden fruit.

He filled the pail with soap and hot water, added the mop then wheeled the bucket to the front room and began putting the chairs on the tabletops. And then Melody began to sing. He froze and listened. She was humming mostly, between the splash of water and the clank of glass against glass, she'd sing a lyric or two, and then go back to the sweetness of hummed music.

Grinning, Tyrrell began to mop. She was born to sing, but had a body meant to fuck. If he had anything to do with it, he'd be the one working that out, his body fully aroused, his emotions already too engaged.

Shit! He chastised himself and got it together. He quickly mopped his way across the room, and then rinsed and cleaned the mop and bucket. Grabbing a couple of rags and special wood soap, he started cleaning off the bar, sticky from spilled cocktails and sodas. He was just about finished when the humming stopped and he heard the sanitize machine turn on.

"Tyrrell, I'm done."

"Yeah," he replied, not looking up from cleaning.

"And I'm soaking wet." Her tone was light and playful.

His gaze flew to her. He'd been working semi-aroused the entire time but her words had him throbbing again. Her dress was soaked. Beneath the wet material, her nipples were pert and obvious. She was wet, but his mouth went dry. The pale-blue satin was dark in the center of her body, and clung to her skin making every line of her body as visible as if she were bare. She didn't wear any panties or he'd have been able to make out the lines.

"Let me get you a towel." *Let me get you naked.*

"That's okay, Tyrrell. I'll change when I get home."

He nodded and she began to saunter toward the stage, her ass swaying side to side as she walked. "I'll just get my purse and get out of your way."

"Melody?"

She glanced back. "Yes, Tyrrell?"

"Do me one more favor before you go?"

"Sure. Anything." She smiled and her amber gaze found his. They were liquid and warm like Hennessey.

He dropped the bar towel and made his way around the countertop. "Sing one more song for me."

She smiled so wide it brightened her eyes. "Of course."

Lifting the bottom of her dress in one hand, she sashayed to the stage, went up the steps and picked up the mic, which was still live. As she always did before she sang, she gripped the mic with both hands. It was metal she touched, but Tyrrell responded like she'd wrapped her delicate fingers around his flesh. Her breath echoed through the speakers.

She turned toward him, her lips damp and slightly parted, her eyes masked with thick lashes, the look on her face pure seduction. He was seduced. His gut tightened like he'd been punched. She was a siren in the fog and he was lost.

After a moment, her lids drifted closed and she began to sing a cappella. Tyrrell recognized the song at once, Jill Scott's "Crown Royal on Ice." Of all the songs, she chose one meant to tease and invite. The lyrics weren't about love, but lust. Melody's intentions were clear and fitting. They were in a bar, and she wanted him. This was the *yes* he'd needed.

She sang the evocative lyrics, of the touch of a hand, the sensual feel of lips and tongue. Her voice silky and meant only for him. He caught her meaning. He was her Crown Royal, smooth and rich and intoxicating. His body hard, his blood on fire, his pulse raging through his veins, he strode across the floor and onto the stage. Her eyes remained closed as she sang, but he stood before her so closely that he could feel her exhale.

More of the seductive lyrics floated from Melody's lips, of thrusting together and being joined so deeply she could breathe for him. She sang on. Her voice was perfect and controlled, but he watched the little pantings of her chest, and the quick rise and fall of her breasts told him she was in the same headspace he was. About to lose control. About to give in to desire. About to soothe lust.

She came to the end of the song, the lyrics wrapping up with a repeat of the chorus. When she finished the final line, Tyrrell spoke. "Breathe for me." He'd whispered, but it echoed through the speakers and filled the room.

Her lids popped open and she gasped like she hadn't realized he'd been so close.

Melody could hardly breathe. Not with Tyrrell standing there, towering over her. He did nothing but stare at her so forcefully she could feel the radiant heat. Her body trembled, only the mic stand kept her anchored and not swaying his direction. She swallowed and wet her lips with her tongue.

He groaned a husky sound of need.

She couldn't wait any longer. "Please," she whispered into the mic.

Pushing the mic out of the way, he closed the distance. One hand went to the back of her neck, his thumb along her jaw; he pulled her forward and tilted her face up. His lips touched hers, a mere sharing of breaths at first. His other hand framed her cheek and drew her closer. He moved his mouth across hers. She swayed, but he supported her.

He made the contact more complete, deepening the kiss. He tasted of beer and passion, of heat and yearning. Of need and fire. And she was melting. Moisture damped her pussy. Her clit swelled. Her inner thighs ached. He claimed her mouth, sliding his tongue along the seam of her lips, then teasing them apart. Opening, she moaned into the feel of him. She'd yearned for him, imagined this kiss time and time again, but every dream she'd dreamt was pale in comparison.

He nibbled her bottom lip with his, the sharp sting of his teeth sending a chill down her spine, the sensation pulling her nipples into tender peaks. And then he pressed farther, touching his tongue to hers, stroking and swirling and thrusting inward.

The kiss was gentle at first. An exploration of lips, of textures. A sharing of passion. There was sweetness in the way he moved his mouth against hers, a tenderness in the way he stroked his tongue into her depths.

She whimpered into his mouth and the kiss changed, shifting to hungry. Urgent and fiery. His hands slid from her cheeks, down her throat, his skin warm and rough. His fingers moved to her shoulders, toyed with the strap of her dress, then smoothed down her naked back where the satin hadn't covered.

"You taste like my favorite song," he mumbled against her mouth before he trailed kisses across her lips, her jawline, down her neck to the sensitive skin below her ear.

She tilted her head giving him more access, her racing pulse thumping where his mouth had been. Putting her arms around his back, she urged him closer. Or hung on. The wetness of her dress smashed between them, her nipples reacting to the coolness of the soaked satin. To the hardness of his muscular chest. To the heat that seeped from his skin and set her body ablaze.

She trembled. But he was there. Supporting her. Holding her. Caressing her. Melody closed her eyes and began to hum. She hummed the pleasure she felt, hummed the emotion she felt but couldn't share.

"Damn, baby," he said, his timbre low and raw. "You're doing things to me." His strong hands curved around her ass as he pulled her forward. "Just your voice." He kissed her mouth, deep and slow. Sultry like a New Orleans July night down by the river.

The length of his hard dick throbbed low on her belly. She felt it to her core. Her clit responded. "Yes, baby," she sang, "baby, please." The random lyrics reverberated through the speakers, bouncing off the empty walls of Margie's empty hole-in-the-wall bar. The sound of their breaths, the tender moans, their throaty groans became a harmony.

"Let me do things to you," he said, breaking the kiss. His tone was low, his voice strained and exigent.

He began stalking forward, forcing her to step backward.

The stage was small. Five steps and she was backed against the baby grand piano. The keys danced out a tune when her butt hit them. But Tyrrell didn't stop. He lifted her up onto the top of the piano, her stiletto heels on the keys. Her knees spread apart as Tyrrell stepped into the *V* of her body.

Placing his palm on her knee, he eased her leg to part her farther, causing the satin of her dress to pool above her thighs. Melody followed his lead, her body responding to his every command, his every touch. Her inner thighs trembled. Arousal seeped from her pussy. Heat sped across her skin; her heart raced.

Bending, he touched his mouth to her inner knee. She could feel him smiling against her skin when she shuddered. He moved slowly, his mouth kissing along her sensitive skin, tongue and teeth leaving a damp trail up her leg to where her body was soaking wet. He pressed two fingers into her welcoming body, spread her lips and claimed her clit with his mouth.

"Ahh..." she cried out. Her heels struck the keys. A-flat. G-sharp. High tones and low. The piano mic had been left on, also, and the room vibrated with the sound of her cries and haphazard beat of the piano's song.

Leaning back, Melody eased onto the piano top and opened her eyes. There was Tyrrell bent between her legs. She reached down and stroked her palm across his head. His short fade tickled against her skin like the prickle from a five-o'-clock shadow.

She arched her back, rotating her hips into his mouth. His fingers worked in her pussy, rubbing, stroking, easing her apart as he tasted her. Warmth and sensation coiled through her core and spread a dusting of prickly heat to fingertips and toes, her clit the center of his attention. His tongue flicked across her delicate peak and then sucked gently just when the tension threatened to uncoil.

"Sing," he murmured against her skin. The vibration of his

words causing her to shake as he licked and teased her. F-minor. B-sharp. A.G. D. B-flat. "Sing for me."

Melody could hardly think, let alone string together lyrics other than the ones she'd been singing that beckoned him to the stage. "Crown Royal on Ice," she began, Jill Scott's words perfectly suited.

Tyrrell's dick throbbed hard. His breathing was shallow. He couldn't take much more. He'd been licking sweet honey from her lips, her body soaking and trembling for him. The piano echoed through the room, mixed with her broken breaths and needy cries. But it was the sound of her singing that almost caused him to nut.

Sucking her clit into his mouth, he flicked his tongue against the flesh as he eased his fingers in and out of her tight flesh. One last lick and she was coming apart in his mouth.

"Tyrrell," she screamed. D. E. A-flat. Her back arched, her delicate fingers tightened where she'd been holding on to the back of his head. "Tyrrell," she sang. She was breathing hard. Her legs shaking as her pussy gripped his fingers and covered him in warm liquid.

Lifting his head, he looked at her face. He'd expected her eyes to be closed, long lashes resting on her perfect latte cheeks. But her eyes were open and watching him. Her amber gaze filled with admiration. And something else.

"Let me breathe for you," she whispered, not breaking the gaze.

His body ached for release. He'd been hard all night. Two seconds were two seconds too long to wait to be inside her right now. He eased himself to a stand, but remained between her spread legs. Her feet struck the keys as he adjusted her knees at his sides. He quickly undid his fly and shoved the jeans off of his hips, his boxers dropping to his ankles.

Her eyes were as warm as Hennessey, her body as wet and as intoxicating. Shifting his hips forward, he gripped his dick in his hand and touched his head to her honey-soaked opening. Her lips surrounded him, urged him deeper. He changed his angle, struggling against his desire, needing this to go slow. Needing it to last longer than a couple of quick strokes.

Her little breathless mews were echoing through the speakers, her ass wiggling at the edge of the piano top as she attempted to ease him inside of her. And then she began to sing. "Please, Tyrrell, please."

And that did it for him. He thrust inside her. Hard. Until she was screaming his name into the mic, the room filled with her fullness and pleasure. Deep. Her walls were slick and tight as she closed around him. Fully seated inside of her, Tyrrell closed his eyes absorbing the velvet texture of her pussy and the sweet scent of her arousal as it floated around them.

She was so tight and so hot and wet. She held him in her grip, and when he thought to go slow, to make it last, she curled her one leg around his back and lifted her hips. The foot remaining on the piano struck several keys. The music nonsensical and amazing.

He thrust in again, pressing against her clit. Out, then in again as a steady rhythm pumped through his system. She grabbed his arms and pulled herself to a sitting position on the edge of the piano. Her nails scraped against his skin, her head arched back, mouth open with breathless whimpers, on a long, slow moan. Leaning forward, he kissed the slender column of her neck, licked her pulse point, ran his tongue over her delicate collarbone.

She worked with him, matching his movements. Thrust her hips upward as he slid his cock inside of her over and over again. She accepted him within her, whimpered on his retreats, cried out as he came into her again. As he ground against her clit. The small bar resounded with their cries and moans.

One of her small hands found the back of his neck and eased him to her mouth. The kiss was tender but urgent. He lavished her lush lips, nipping and nibbling as he worked his dick into her sultry depths. And she was riding back on him, taking his solid length into her body, angling her hips as he thrust back in.

She was shaking again and he could feel the flutter of her pussy walls against his dick. Knew she was about to come again. He claimed her mouth with his, capturing her singing in his throat. And came as she did. His body jerked and emptied. The piano sang as they trembled in each other's arms, the speakers announcing their climax. The kiss ended and her slight body went limp against his chest, supported by his embrace.

They were still for a while, still connected, still shaking, still breathing the shallow pants. He held her, stroked her back, rubbed a gentle thumb across her cheek. "Thank you," he whispered. "Thank you for singing for me."

He felt her smile against his shirt. "I've been waiting for you to ask."

"For real?" Surprised, his chest welling with pride.

"I learned the lyrics just for you." She turned her head and kissed his chest.

There was something so sweet and emotional about her kiss.

"You'll sing for me again?"

She replied without hesitation. "Whenever you want me to."

He laughed. "How about tonight. Tomorrow. The night after that?" He pressed his lips to her temple. "How about every night."

She wiggled. "How about now." And she began to sing.

# OFF THE BEATEN PATH

Heidi Champa

"We've been walking for over an hour. It's time to give up and admit we're lost."

"We're not lost. I know exactly where we are. Stop worrying so much, Kelsey."

I was ready to punch Tony when I heard his smug words. The hike we were on had been his idea and when we first got underway, I was on board. It was a gorgeous day, the first one of the spring, and all I wanted to do was get outside. Tony suggested a nice hike at a nearby and familiar trail and I quickly agreed. We'd filled our backpacks and grabbed our walking sticks and piled into the car for the fifteen-minute drive to one of our favorite spots. The views along the trail were always spectacular and for the first hour of the hike, I was really enjoying myself. Until Tony decided he wanted to take a different path, one that neither of us had ever walked before. He swore up and down that he knew where he was going and that it would be worth it to do something different.

I'd agreed, overwhelmed with the idea of having an adventure. But after walking for what felt like forever through thorny bushes, getting my feet wet trying to cross a stream and being bitten by a few bugs, I was more than ready to call it a day. The trouble was, we were in the middle of the woods. And, despite his protests, we were, in fact, lost. We backtracked several times, retracing our steps to find some landmark he swore would lead us to the right spot, wherever the hell that was. It didn't take long for me to get frustrated and soon our tranquil day had me in the midst of a tension headache. I had kept quiet, for the most part, but I was starting to get fed up. I decided to let Tony know, in the hopes it would make him see reason and turn around.

"You don't know where we are any more than I do. I haven't seen one of those little blue dashes marking the trail for at least a half hour. And we keep going down the hill, when according to the map you showed me before, we're supposed to be heading up."

I sighed as I hefted my backpack, trying to make myself more comfortable. I could almost feel the blisters forming on my toes as my left hiking boot rubbed the side of my big toe. We passed a huge mass of boulders that I was sure I'd seen before and I sighed again. It was getting more and more difficult to maintain my composure; my heart was pounding, and it wasn't from the exertion. His next sentence only inflamed me more.

"You know, hiking is a lot less fun when you're like this."

I wanted to throw something at him, but there was nothing nearby that would do the trick. I tried to keep my voice calm, but even I could hear the tension around the edges of my words.

"Well, I'm sorry. But being chipper is beyond me right now. I'm tired and I'm getting cranky."

"Getting? I'd say we're already there, wouldn't you?"

He said it with a chuckle, but I poked him with my walking

stick anyway, too annoyed to appreciate his attempt at humor.

"Fine. I'm cranky. Sue me. If I'd known we were going to be traipsing around indefinitely, I would have brought more snacks. I think some chocolate would go a long way to improving my mood. But we didn't bring any."

He stopped and turned around, putting his hands on my shoulders.

"Listen, baby, I promise you, I know where we are, and I know where we're going. It's not that much farther. You just have to trust me."

I smirked at him, trying to keep my sarcastic response from spilling out of my mouth. I'd heard him say things like this before. Usually before a disastrous kitchen mishap or wasted hours driving in circles. I bit my tongue.

"Fine. I trust you. But I'm warning you. Another hour of this and I can't be held responsible for my actions."

"Noted."

He spun on his heel and we kept walking, the terrain growing more intense and the brush we had to trudge through getting thicker. My toes were sore from being smashed against the front of my boots, my legs burning from trying not to fall forward down the steep descent. Pebbles skidded down the hill as my feet slid a little bit and I reached out to steady myself on a tree.

"Jesus, Tony. Where the hell are you taking me?"

"We're so close. Just hang in there for a few more minutes."

Suddenly, the trail leveled off and we walked along a beautiful stream, the water rushing loudly over the rocks. We followed the path a bit longer, the smell of wet earth filling my nose. Tony stopped in front of me and when I looked past him into the clearing, my mouth fell open. There, in front of us, was a waterfall, emptying into a pool that looked gorgeous and cool.

"See I told you it would be worth it."

I took in the view, taking the opportunity to take my pack off and stretch my back a bit. Tony's hands started kneading my tight shoulder muscles and I closed my eyes for a moment.

"Okay, fine. It was worth it. This is really amazing."

He leaned in and put his mouth right next to my ear.

"Wanna go swimming?"

His arms went around my waist and pulled me close, his chest pressing into my back.

"You're not serious."

"Why not? The water looks amazing, don't you think?"

I turned around and looked at him. He was smiling and when I met his eyes, he waggled his eyebrows.

"Yeah, it does, but..."

"But what?"

"We don't have our bathing suits."

He spun me around and kissed me hard. By the time he pulled back, I was out of breath.

"We don't need them. Do we?"

Tony kissed me again and as much as it pained me to do it, I tried to remain practical.

"I guess not. But we don't have towels either."

He grinned and reached for his backpack, opening the zipper with a flourish.

"What if I told you that we did have towels?"

"We do?"

"Yup. And, sunscreen."

I smiled at him, my resolve slowly disappearing.

"You planned this the whole time, didn't you?"

He nodded, wrapping his arms around me again.

"I did. Well, I didn't plan to be hiking for so long. Since I'm being honest, I should tell you, we were a little bit lost up there. But we ended up in the right place, so no harm done."

He kissed me and I felt his hands steal under my T-shirt. Before I could protest, he pulled it over my head and tossed it aside. I instinctually looked around to make sure no one could see me. Even though we hadn't passed a single person on our hike, I was sure now that I was topless, a group of people would show up.

"I'm not sure about this, Tony."

"Oh, come on, Kels. It'll be fun. If it helps sweeten the deal, I may have some chocolate in my bag."

"You've been holding out on me this whole time? Bastard."

He laughed and shucked off his own T-shirt. The sight of his bare chest made my breath catch, even after all these years. I reached out and touched his sweaty skin, easing myself against him.

"Sorry. But it was all part of my romantic plan. I thought it might be nice. You know, for after."

I looked into his hazel eyes and my fingers dropped to the button on his shorts. As I eased the zipper down, he leaned in and kissed me.

"You really don't play fair at all, you know that," I said with a smile.

"Yeah, but it's more fun this way."

We made quick work of stripping off the rest of our clothes. Tony didn't bother to wait for me, jumping into the pool of water with abandon. It was just like him. When he resurfaced, he threw his wet hair back and beckoned me with a crooked finger.

"Come on. I'm waiting."

I walked gingerly over a few rocks and slowly waded into the water, letting out a gasp as the cool water touched my sensitive skin. My feet skimmed over the stones at the bottom and I let my head sink under the water, staying submerged for a long moment. When I came up for air, Tony wrapped me in his arms. and pulled me to him. I felt my tired muscles starting to relax as we floated together, the water feeling so unbelievably good. He nibbled my earlobe before whispering in my ear.

"Remember the last time we did this?"

I thought back to the early days of our relationship, when we went skinny-dipping in our neighbor's pool while they were out of town.

"This is a way nicer place than the Anderson's aboveg-round."

"I agree. The waterfall is a nice touch, isn't it?"

I didn't have time to answer, because Tony pulled us both under the stream of water, the cool liquid pounding down on us. He moved us a few feet until we were behind the wall of water, our laughter echoing off the stone surrounding us. I wrapped my legs around his body and kissed him, enjoying the slippery feel of his skin against mine.

"I'm sorry for being cranky earlier. If you'd told me we were going to do this, I might have been in a better mood."

"That would have spoiled the surprise. Although it would have made the trip here a bit more tolerable."

I splashed him, but he retaliated by kissing me hard. His hands slid up my back and down again, cupping my ass. I felt his cock harden against my leg, things between us heating up quickly. His hands moved around to my breasts and I gasped into his mouth when his thumbs started toying with my nipples. I felt the heat growing between my legs, my body hungry for more. Reaching down between us, I took him in hand, stroking his hard dick until he moaned. His tongue dove deep into my mouth, quieting my cries of pleasure. He kissed my neck before resting his forehead against mine.

"Maybe we should get out."

"Already?"

He chuckled, stroking my wet hair back.

"We can always get back in later. But, right now, I want you too much to wait."

He didn't even give me the chance to respond as he carried me through the waterfall, back out into the open. After we toweled off as best we could, Tony spread out a small blanket that was somehow hidden in his backpack. He was so rarely sneaky; I had to smile at all the planning he'd done. Tony sat down on the blanket and I joined him, but he quickly pulled me into his lap. The sun felt warm on my skin, the cool water still dripping from my hair running down my back. Tony kissed me, but he didn't stay on my mouth for long. His kisses traveled down my neck to my chest, his hand cupping my breast before he wrapped his lips around my nipple. I arched my back, looking up to the sky as he swirled his tongue around and around, giving a sucking pull before moving on to the other one.

I twined my fingers in his damp hair and held him close, relishing the sweet torture of his mouth. My pussy was wet and I took his hand and moved it there so he could feel how excited I was. His fingers slid over my slit for a moment before one slipped inside me, making me cry out. He added another and I rocked against him as he pressed his palm against my clit, the friction exquisite.

"Lie down, Kelsey."

I didn't want to move out of his arms, but I did as he asked, stretching myself out on the blanket. He kissed me before moving his mouth between my legs, his tongue laving over my clit in small circles. His fingers were back inside me and I moaned along with the noise of the water. The tree branches danced in the wind and I no longer cared if anyone happened to see us. In that moment, the only thing I could think about was Tony. My thighs started to tremble just as his tongue stopped its teasing dance. He crawled over me and kissed me sweetly, the head of his cock resting against my wet pussy.

"God, I love you, baby."

"I love you too, Tony."

His name was barely out of my mouth when he entered me, my legs wrapping around his back.

"Fuck, you feel so good."

He'd said it to me a million times before, but the words always made my stomach lurch and my pussy clench. I held on to his strong shoulders as he fucked me, slow and hard. Tony looked at me, our eyes locked for a long moment before he kissed me, our still slick bodies moving together effortlessly. He moaned in my ear as I kissed his neck, just the way he liked, the sound of him nothing short of intoxicating. It had been forever since we'd done it outside, or really anywhere outside the bedroom. Everything about it was overwhelming, all my senses felt like they were turned up a bit. Each stroke of him inside me had me groaning and squirming, the edge getting dangerously close. I reached down and gripped his ass, urging him on, my body desperate for release.

"Tony, I'm so close."

He practically growled as he pounded into me faster, my orgasm as powerful as any I'd ever had. I could hear my voice echoing through the trees, my body slowly relaxing as the waves of pleasure started to ebb. Tony came just as fiercely, his whole body shaking above me until every muscle went slack and I felt the full weight of him on top of me.

Slowly, things returned to normal and he rolled away, both of us looking up at the perfect blue sky. He was still panting a bit as he spoke.

"Holy shit, that was amazing."

"My thoughts exactly."

He pulled me close, kissing the top of my head. We lay in silence for a long time, letting the sounds of nature take over, the rush of the water behind us making my eyes grow heavy. Just as I was about to drift off, a thought popped into my head. I propped up on my elbow and looked at him. He shielded his eyes from the sun and furrowed his brow.

"Why are you looking at me like that?"

I ran my hand down his chest and put on my best coy smile.

"Someone promised me chocolate."

# FAIR GAME

## Crystal Jordan

"Hello, Gillian."

She cradled the phone between her shoulder and ear, a surprised smile curling her lips. Her body warmed at the sound of his voice through the line, deep and a little rough. It had been a long time since she'd heard from him. Months. She used to see him in the library at least once a week, and she'd enjoyed it far more than she should have. "Hello, Robert. Or do you want me to call you Dr. Smith now?"

"Robert. You'll *always* call me Robert." As if he realized he'd been a little more forceful than necessary, he cleared his throat. "I only make my students and colleagues I don't like refer to me by my formal title."

He'd been in his last year of graduate school when she'd become a librarian at this university. The chemistry had sparked the moment she met him, more intense than anything she'd ever experienced. But there'd been multiple issues that stood between her and the ability to scratch that particular itch. Still, she'd missed having him around since he'd transitioned from grad student to professor.

"Um...you wouldn't happen to have a moment to see if the library has access to a particular journal article, would you?"

"Of course, let me check for you." Tapping the keyboard on her computer, she brought up the library's website and clicked on the proper link. "What's the journal and article title, what year was it published and who wrote it?"

"Sorry, I only have a partial citation. It's from 1987 by a J. Doyle. *The Journal of Sexuality*. I'm doing some research on female arousal."

Hearing the words *sexuality* and *female arousal* roll off of his tongue made her insides tighten as she typed in the information. She'd had far too many arousing sexual thoughts about him and had wished for a long time that she could turn those fantasies into reality, but she'd never been good at being bold with men and flirting. She'd always been too cautious and too inclined to overthink every possible consequence.

So, instead of making a naughty comeback about how she'd like to help him with his investigation into exactly what aroused females—her, specifically—she sighed softly and tucked a lock of hair behind her ear. "You know how to do these kinds of searches. I showed you."

"Yeah, you caught me." He huffed out a laugh. "I was just calling to see how you are."

Surprised excitement buzzed within her. He was checking up on her. Nice.

"I'm...good." Maybe she didn't have to initiate too much; maybe just getting him into her office again was enough. It was a start, right? A slow grin formed on her lips. "We only have that journal in print, down in the lower level stacks. I can pull it for you and photocopy the article. Why don't you come by and pick it up after your last class today?"

"Come by your office, or are you leaving it at the front desk?" Something in his tone sharpened, made her belly quiver.

"My office." She squeezed her eyes closed. "I've been hoping you'd call with another...request."

"Oh?"

"Yes." She hesitated, steeled her nerves. "You never come by the library to see me anymore."

He was silent so long, she wasn't sure he'd respond at all. "I didn't think my attentions were welcome."

"They are," she said quietly. It was a huge thing to say that out loud, to admit to anyone except herself.

"I thought you were dating someone."

"We broke up." She twisted the phone cord around her finger. "Over Christmas break last year."

Her relationship had withered within six months of moving here, so she could have pursued something with Robert, but why? He was about to graduate and head off for a new job. She'd seen how well she did with long distance and she wasn't interested in trying again.

"Christmas was *ten months ago*." An edge of incredulousness filled his tone. "Why didn't you tell me? You wanted me—I know you did. And I was crawling the damn walls wanting you. I fantasized about sliding inside of you so often I had a permanent hard-on, and you're telling me we could have been together *all* of last semester and you didn't say a word?"

"No, I didn't." She wanted to take offense at his tone, but her mind couldn't stop repeating *fantasized about sliding inside of you*. Yes. She wanted that, had since the moment they'd met. "There were a lot of reasons. I wasn't ready for anything right after and then..."

"Then?"

"You were a student at the university I *work* for. It just seemed wrong and unprofessional, which isn't the way to come across during the first year at a job." She dropped her head into her hand, closing her eyes. "And...and I thought you were going away after you graduated. So, I..."

"I get it." He sighed into the phone, and the line crackled. "But I didn't go away. I took a position here. So where does that leave us now?"

"Now." She sat back in her chair, letting a slow breath ease out. "Come pick up the article and...maybe we can go to dinner?"

There wouldn't be even a hint of impropriety about dating a faculty member. He was fair game.

And since she was single now, she was fair game, too. If he was still interested.

She hoped he was still very, very interested. She knew she was.

A pained chuckle rippled through the phone. "I don't just want dinner with you tonight. I've been waiting for over a *year*, and I want more."

She licked her lips, her heart tripping against her ribs. "Me, too."

"Prove it."

It was a blatant challenge, and one she didn't want to back down from. She'd craved him for so long she ached. "How?"

The sound he made was somewhere between a hum of anticipation and a groan. "What are you wearing?"

"Um...a camisole and cardigan and one of those knee-length skirts that bells out and kind of swishes when I move. Nothing fancy." Or particularly sexy, but she hadn't known she'd be going on a date tonight.

"So the skirt isn't tight?"

"Sorry, no." She smoothed a palm down the floral-patterned fabric. "Not at all."

"Good." Amusement and something sinful filled his voice. "Then it shouldn't be difficult to slide your panties off for me."

"Right now?" The very idea stunned her, sent lust spiraling straight to her core. The walls of her pussy clenched once, hard.

"Yes."

Her breath rushed in swift little pants, and her nipples hardened. Could she really do this? She was at the library! Her hand gripped the edge of the desk until her knuckles turned white. Panic ricocheted through her before reason set in, and she dragged in a steadying lungful of air. Who would ever know? Just her. And Robert. Her office door was closed and locked. Excitement bolted within her. She set a hand on her knee, easing her skirt up so she could slide her fingers under the waistband of her panties. Lifting her hips off her chair, she slipped the scrap of cotton down her legs until it pooled around her ankles. Oh, Jesus. She'd actually done it. Her heart pounded, blood rushing through her veins. She stepped out of her underwear and quickly stuffed them into the very bottom of her purse. "Okay."

A low, pleasured growl filled her ear. "Are you wet?"

"Y-yes." God, she was soaking. She could feel the slickness coating the lips of her pussy, and she squeezed her thighs together to savor the throb between them.

"I want more, Gillian." His voice was no more than a deep rumble now, the pitch alone enough to make her body react. "I want you to touch yourself."

The breath stopped in her lungs, shock and lust twining together within her. Impossibly, inevitably, she grew damper. Reaching under her skirt again, she brushed her hand over her curls. Her body trembled, her nerves stretching taut at the idea of doing this in her office. It was unprofessional, wrong and amazingly hot. This was insane.

"Play with your clit, slide your fingers into your pussy," he urged, and that was all it seemed to take to make her throw whatever was left of her caution aside. The bottom line was, she wanted this, wanted him.

Slipping her fingertips between her slick folds, she teased her hot flesh. Her clit hardened, blooming against her palm as she rubbed herself in slow circles. Sweat beaded on her forehead, and her breathing sped to pants. She closed her eyes, letting the sensations take her. She stroked up and down her wet slit, and her pussy clenched on emptiness. Rolling a thumb over her clitoris sent lightning shooting through her pelvis.

She moaned softly. God, she hoped no one walked by her office. The door might be shut, but that wouldn't stop them from hearing things they shouldn't.

"Fuck yourself with your fingers, Gillian. Hard and fast," he ordered, and she could hear his rough desperation, his need. For her.

Biting her lip, she whimpered. She arched into her hand, plunging two fingers deep into her sex. The rhythm she set was swift. Tingles broke over her limbs, and her muscles quivered. She added a third finger, relishing the stretch. So close. She was so close, and knowing he was listening to every hitch of her breath, every low moan, just made her burn even hotter. Slamming her digits into her pussy, she ground the heel of her palm against her clit and climax crashed over her in a blistering rush. Her channel contracted in waves, and her mouth opened in a silent scream. Shudders passed through her, and it took long moments for her to relax back into her chair, spent.

"Did you come?" The warmth in his tone made her heart squeeze.

"God, yes," she gasped. "Really hard."

"Very good, sweetheart." His chuckle was strained. "I'm going to be harder than steel for the rest of the day. I'm through with classes, but I have one more meeting. Right now, in fact. But after that..."

He didn't finish, but he didn't have to. She knew what would happen tonight, and she doubted dinner was on the menu. Did she care? Not even a little. This had been building for a long time, and she *needed* to know exactly what it was like to touch him, to taste him, to fuck him.

"I'll be here, waiting for you," she said. Then she gave a low chuckle. "Is it bad to *like* that you'll be harder than steel for me? It does a lot for stimulating my female arousal."

"You're killing me, sweetheart." He gave a helpless groan. "I'll be there in a little while. I've missed you. Seeing you, being near you."

"I've missed you too. So much." Her smile was slow and soft. "Come to me as soon as you can."

"I will," he promised.

She tugged her skirt down, her body feeling languorous. Shutting her eyes for a moment, she let herself imagine what it would be like to have his hands on her skin, to have him stroke her the way she'd stroked herself. A shiver ran through her.

The phone started beeping in her hands, letting her know Robert had disconnected. It jolted her back to reality. She hung up and glanced around her office, discomfited. What now? She had time to kill and there was no chance she could focus on real work. Her gaze lit on the computer screen. Well, she could get the article he wanted, though he'd admitted that wasn't the real reason for his call. She shrugged. It would give her something to do so she wouldn't drive herself crazy.

She unbuttoned her cardigan and pulled it off so she was

left in a silk and lace camisole. A bit too revealing to wear by itself to work, but she wouldn't mind if it gave Robert some ideas. She grinned as she stood, draping the cardi over the back of her chair. The brush of air against her sex as she moved made her cheeks heat with a blush, but she resisted the urge to slip her panties back on. This was how Robert wanted her, and she'd been running from him for too long. Worse, she'd been running from herself. She'd had her reasons, but they were gone now.

It only took a few minutes to ride the elevator down to the lower level, which was the library's kind way of referring to the basement. They kept their microfilm collection and all of their old journals down here. Tables lined the wide walkway between the tall metal stacks, and a few students sat studying. The carpet muffled her footsteps as she strode through the quiet space, searching for the right shelf.

There. She turned into the aisle and walked her fingers along the spines of the volumes until she found the 1987 bound edition of *The Journal of Sexuality*. She had just begun to slide it off the shelf when a masculine hand reached around her to grab it. Jolting, she twisted to look back and found Robert.

God, he was handsome. It struck her hard, after months of not seeing him. His dark hair curled over his forehead, and his eyes were a piercing blue that a pair of wire-rimmed glasses couldn't disguise. High cheekbones and a square jaw made his face angular. Small dimples formed in his cheeks when he smiled down at her.

Her mouth dried and it took her a moment to find words. "What are you doing here?"

One of his eyebrows arched, and his eyes crinkled at the corners. He stepped even closer to her, his front to her back, until it felt as if he surrounded her with his body heat. "I do know how to find a journal. You showed me, remember?"

She snorted. "You know what I meant."

His hands closed over her shoulders, pulling her toward him, and she could feel the length of his erection prodding her buttocks. Her sex throbbed with need, fire pooling in her belly.

"I canceled the meeting. I couldn't wait to see you." He nuzzled the back of her neck, then bit her nape. "What if you had changed your mind again before I got here?"

The pained edge to his voice pierced her with regret. Denying the feelings between them—and not just the sexual ones—had hurt more than just her. She'd hurt him, too, by pushing him away. Remorse cinched around her heart. "I won't change my mind, Robert. I've always known what I wanted, I just didn't think I could or should have it. I wasn't—"

"Shh." His fingers tightened on her arms, a comforting squeeze. "If you want to see where this goes, then we don't have to hash everything out right this second. We have time."

When he slid his tongue up the side of her neck, she shuddered, her nipples peaking. "Yes, we have time. A lot of it."

Crooking an arm around her waist, he held her in place while he bit down lightly on her earlobe. "Then we should start enjoying it, shouldn't we?"

Her chuckle was low, husky. "I already did."

She felt him smile against her skin. "Ah, yes. When we were discussing my study of female arousal earlier."

His palm flattened against her stomach, inching upward until he could curve his hand over her breast.

"You're not wearing a bra." There was delight in his tone.

"I've never needed one." Her mind shut down, unable to form another coherent thought as his fingers learned the shape of her breast, circled the hardened crest. Clinging to sanity, she managed to force out words that might stop him.

"There are security cameras in the library, Dr. Smith."

She tilted her head, indicating the dark little dome embedded in the ceiling that covered the camera.

He spared it a mere glance before he maneuvered them so his back was to it, shielding them from its view. Now all she could see were the shelves and the wall at the far end of the stacks. Then he rubbed a thumb over her nipple and she didn't care what she was looking at, just what he was doing with his very talented fingers.

He whispered in her ear, "I believe I told you to always call me Robert."

"What if I don't *always* do what you say?" She deliberately wiggled her backside against his cock.

"You don't have to, of course. Then again...are you hoping to be punished?" There was laughter behind the words, but his hand tightened on her breast, almost to the point of pain but not quite. The intensity of the sensation brought her up on her tiptoes. "Do you enjoy being spanked?"

Heat flooded her face, as well as other parts of her anatomy. She felt a bead of moisture slip from her sex, and she squeezed her legs together to halt its slide. "Sometimes."

He hissed in a breath, a shudder wracking his body. She felt his cock twitch against her ass, and she couldn't resist. Reaching back, she wedged a hand between them so she could stroke him through his slacks. The angle was awkward, but she didn't care. His hips rolled forward to press into her palm, and she squeezed the long, solid length of him. His free hand groped down to gather her skirt up. Shock robbed her of breath when he dipped into her sex, flicking a fingertip over her clit. Her thighs jerked, and need exploded within her. Just that quick touch, and she was on the edge of orgasm. Her grip tightened convulsively on his dick, and he groaned in response.

A sputter of laughter from the next aisle over slapped her back to the real world and where they were.

"Students," she whispered.

For just a moment, she wasn't quite sure if that would stop him, if he'd already been pushed too far, but then he withdrew his fingers and let her skirt drop. "Let's go back to your office. *Now.*"

She bobbed her chin in a rapid nod, turning to rush toward the elevator. Every step made her legs brush together, increasing her agony and reminding her how desperately she wanted to come. He strode beside her, near enough that their arms brushed as they moved. That only sharpened her need. Several students got into the elevator with them, which was probably a blessing since it kept them from going at it in the small, enclosed space. She had to remind herself that there were security cameras in the elevators, too. The entire library had them, with the sole exception of the librarians' personal offices. Which meant this elevator needed to *hurry up* so they could have a little more privacy.

Robert met her gaze over the heads of a pair of gossiping sorority girls, a little smile tugging at his lips. The expression was tender and rueful at the same time and made emotions bubble up that she'd shoved into the deepest corner of her soul long ago. She'd felt guilty, shamed, for desiring him. First because of her boyfriend and then because of her job, and it was so amazing to be free of restraints. She offered him a grin in return, feeling happier than she had in quite a while. She was exactly where she wanted to be and with exactly who she wanted. Well, she'd rather be in her office already, but Robert was definitely the company she wanted to keep.

She pushed back a lock of hair that had fallen forward over her breast, the auburn color gleaming under the fluorescent lights. His brilliant blue gaze followed the movement, lingering for a moment too long on her chest. Heat burst inside her again, and she felt a keen rush of relief when they finally arrived on the correct floor. She exited with him hot on her heels.

Opening the door to the administrative area of the library, she led the way to her office, weaving through a maze of corridors and cubicles. They turned the last corner, and his palm on her low back urged her to hurry.

"Gillian, hello." A petite woman drew up short at the sight of them, her gaze dropping to where Robert's hand touched her. "Who's this?"

"Marta." She smiled at the other woman and took a small step away from Robert. "This is Dr. Smith, from the Anthropology Department. Robert, this is the dean of the library, Marta Kaufer."

He offered the dean a grin. "It's a pleasure to meet you. The library has a wonderful collection in my area of study."

Marta's arms were loaded with several thick folders, which kept her from trying to shake his hand. Good thing, considering where his fingers had just been. Gillian hoped her cheeks hadn't turned bright red, but she suspected they had.

The dean frowned. "But Gillian works with our Sociology Department."

"I know." Robert's smile broadened, and he curled a possessive arm around Gillian's waist to begin drawing her toward her office. "If you'll excuse us."

They left Marta staring after them, and Gillian sighed. "That wasn't very subtle."

He grunted. "If you're in this, you're in all the way. No more pretending we don't want each other."

"I don't want to pretend, but we're—"

"Good." He pushed her inside her office and shut and locked the door behind them. "Because that's nonnegotiable for me. I don't lie or hide when I'm with someone, and that's what I want from you. We're totally out of the closet with this."

"Okay," she whispered. It could all go wrong, dating a colleague could blow up in her face, but she had to deal with that. She could let things get in her way or she could accept the risk and hope for the best. She cleared her throat, made her voice prim. "As long as 'totally out of the closet' doesn't mean shagging in the public areas of the library. I do have *some* professional standards to uphold, you know."

"The privacy of your office works." He flashed a dazzling smile, tugged off his glasses and set them on a bookshelf by the door. Then he advanced on her like a predator hunting his prey.

Heart racing, she backed up until she hit the wall. He loomed above her, his gaze sliding over her body, and flames licked at her core. She grabbed the collar of his polo shirt and pulled him down for a kiss. Their first.

Damn, the man could *kiss*. He pinned her in place and used his whole body, rubbing against her, his cock settling in the crook of her thighs, his hands sliding over her. She wrapped her arms around his neck, shoving her tongue into his mouth. The taste of him was perfect. Coffee and something sweet—caramel. Hot, sugary caramel. It was addicting, intoxicating. He moved down to brush his lips over her jaw and graze his teeth over the sensitive spot at the base of her throat.

"Robert, please."

"I will." He lifted his head to wink at her. "Please you, that is."

Dropping to his knees, he swept her skirt up and pushed it into her hands.

"Hold this," he ordered, and she obeyed, sliding her legs apart to give him as much access as he wanted. His fingers parted the lips of her sex, and she flushed at being so exposed, at having him look at her pussy.

His lips closed over her clit, and she mewled, all thought fleeing her mind. He stabbed two big fingers into her sex, pumping them into her hot, slick channel. The pace he set was swift and rough and maddening. Curling his tongue around her clitoris, he drove her to the edge of sanity. She clamped her mouth shut, stifling the scream that threatened to spill out. Her sex clenched around his fingers, and when he bit at her sensitive flesh, it catapulted her into orgasm. She shivered, her fingers fisting in her skirt as she shook with each wave of climax that rocked her.

She sagged against the wall when it was over, her heart thudding in her chest, her breath rushing in broken gasps.

He grabbed the bottom of her camisole as he stood and pulled it over her head. The sound of need he made sent lust spiraling through her. He closed a big hand over her breast, rubbing his thumb over the tip. A grin curled the corners of his lips as he watched her nipple tighten for him. Dipping forward, he sucked it between his lips, battling it with his tongue, shoving it hard against the roof of his mouth.

And just that quickly she needed more, craved it. The bliss of orgasm gave way to a sharp spike of desire. He gave her other breast the same treatment, and she pressed her palm over her mouth to cover the low keening that broke from her throat.

He let her nipple slide from his mouth, and tugged his polo off, tossing it aside. She immediately reached out to touch him, sliding her fingers into the crisp hair on his chest and toying with his flat nipples. They beaded for her and she wanted to lick and bite them.

"No," he growled. "I'm not going to last much longer, and if you touch me, I might actually come in my pants."

He lifted her up and laid her across her desk, need flushing his face and drawing his skin taut across his high cheekbones. He drew her ankles up and set them against his shoulders. The harsh rasp of his zipper was loud in the small room, and he procured a condom from god-knew-where, sheathing his erection quickly. She stilled at the blunt probing of his cock at her slick entrance. The stretch was divine.

"You have no idea how many times I've fantasized about fucking you just like this, spread out across your desk." His breathing was ragged as he hilted himself inside her pussy. "You're so beautiful, Gillian."

She rocked her hips upward, meeting his thrusts. He was big, thick enough that it might have hurt to take all of him if she hadn't been so wet. As it was, she quivered on the edge of exquisite pleasured-pain. He braced his hands on her thighs, holding her close as he picked up speed. Every plunge took him deep and made his pelvis smack against her clit. Starbursts exploded behind her eyelids, and the muscles in her belly tightened as orgasm shimmered just beyond her reach. She covered her breasts with her fingers, teasing her nipples. The fire that flashed in his gaze as he watched her made her burn hotter. Her sex tightened around his cock, and she moaned. He fucked her harder, shoving her even closer to climax.

"Come for me, Gillian. Now."

There was no choice. Her back bowed against the desk, and her pussy convulsed on his dick, orgasm hitting her in a tsunami wave that dragged her under. Her sex milked the length of his erection, and each time he pistoned into her, another wave of climax crashed over her. It went on forever, left her sobbing with the power of it.

Groaning, his grip tightened painfully on her legs. He hammered into her until he froze, shuddering out his own climax.

His sharp gaze grew hazy as he came, and he ground down on her clit, sending aftershocks of orgasm shivering through her body. He hung there for a long moment before he collapsed over her, resting his forehead between her breasts, his breath cooling her sweat-dampened skin. She hugged him close. Tingles still rippled over her limbs, and a grin spread across her face.

It had been even better than she expected, and her hopes had been pretty high. Amazing.

"Ready for dinner?" He lifted his head to meet her gaze, a little smile playing over his lips.

A chuckle spilled out of her. "We've definitely worked up an appetite."

His eyes narrowed, focusing on her nipple, less than an inch from his face. "On second thought, let's do takeout and go to my place. Feel like a sleepover?"

"Yes." To everything. Whatever he had in mind, she was in. "In case I forget to mention it later, I'm really glad you called today." Her grin widened when he laughed. "And I assume it's fair game to call *you* tomorrow and put in a request. Maybe do a little study of my own on how to stimulate male arousal?"

"Oh, yeah. It's totally fair game, sweetheart." His gaze danced with mirth, but his expression was solemn. "Though I imagine the study is going to take a long time to complete. Years, in fact."

"We have time to experiment. Lots of it."

# LATE BLOOMERS

Annabeth Leong

The day after her second wedding anniversary, Sheila realized she hadn't been in love with her husband when they got married. Of course, she'd thought she was in love. She had said the words back to him with assurance on the night he'd first said them to her because she'd liked him a whole lot and hadn't wanted to break up.

Rather than igniting passion in her, however, Charles had simply made sense as a partner. Her parents loved him, they had compatible political views and their fights always resolved reasonably, amicably. Sheila occasionally felt jealous of people such as her friend, Amy, who conducted a series of burning affairs with visiting lecturers at the college where she worked as an adjunct professor. Those always ended badly, though, and Sheila preferred having Charles steadily at her side.

Many times she had told herself that what she had with Charles *was* love, and that the seismic feelings Amy liked to express were some sort of delusion. That idea didn't hold water anymore now that Sheila was trembling, glancing at the clock on the dashboard of her car, desperate to get through traffic and come home to him even though she'd just seen him that morning.

She tried to calm herself by going over the events of the night before.

They had decided to stay in for their anniversary to save a little money, and Sheila had sipped a glass of red wine, and sautéed asparagus while Charles grilled steaks out on the patio. Occasionally, she had glanced at him through the glass door—admiring the smooth fit of his slacks, the sharp, precise cut of his bristly black hair, the lean muscle that rippled across his back.

When had he gotten so good-looking? When they'd started dating, it had seemed like nerdy destiny, the two bespectacled Asians in the English department winding up together. Now, his glasses had a keen, stylish shape, and he stood over the grill with sleek confidence. Her heart had fluttered, and a tongue of flame had licked down her belly and settled between her legs.

The buzz of arousal was slight but impossible to ignore. Sheila couldn't remember having felt it spontaneously before. Faint, related sensations had sometimes come to her on nights when Charles really worked at it, but for the most part, Sheila had always believed passion was for other people.

By the time he'd come in with the steaks, she'd been flustered, nervous, unable to stop smiling. "This is nice," she'd said when they sat down to dinner, and had immediately gotten angry with herself for failing to express what she was feeling.

"It is," Charles had replied, pulling her in for a quick kiss.

The contact had been over almost before it began, much too quickly. Sheila had taken a long swallow of her wine, but the burn of the alcohol was nothing compared to the lingering heat on her cheek where his lips had been. For the rest of dinner, she had fantasized about what it would be like to tell him with her body what she couldn't with her words. She had wanted to grab his shirt collar to keep him from pulling away, to climb into his lap and make him kiss her.

They'd had sex after dinner, in the half-apologetic way that had become their habit, but his touch had seemed different. Sheila had clenched her jaw to keep her teeth from audibly chattering, and when he'd entered her, she had wanted something that she didn't know how to ask for.

In the morning, she had felt as if they'd just met. Suddenly, she was living with a handsome stranger. This wasn't only the Charles who left a cup of coffee on the counter for her every morning, or the Charles who read the news on his tablet computer over breakfast while she skimmed advice columns. This was someone fascinating, a man she wanted to know, to touch. To love, in a way that Sheila now understood she'd never experienced.

Still caught in traffic, she clenched her hands tighter around the steering wheel. Marriage agreed with her. She treasured the shared daily activities—sleeping together, waking together, greeting each other at home in the evenings. In the two years since their wedding, those things had taken on unexpected depth for her, weighted with care.

In the first year, she had taken this in stride. There was supposed to be a honeymoon period, and if that hadn't included sex on the kitchen table, at least there had been happiness. As time went on, however, Sheila had begun to feel surprised that her feelings were growing, not lessening. Friends had told her about falling into a rut, taking their spouses for granted, operating like two ships passing in the night. Sheila, on the other hand, had been increasingly aware of Charles. She'd looked forward more and more to holding him at night, the heat of his back radiating against her chest.

Had she begun to fall—really fall—for him? Sheila wasn't sure if she should feel embarrassed or exhilarated. On the one hand, she felt like a fool for having taken so long to notice the man she'd married. On the other hand, fragile new desires were beginning to form, and the thought of satisfying them with Charles made her heart pound.

Her drive home had never seemed so long, though she arrived ten minutes earlier than usual. Sheila fumbled with the keys in the door, trying to plan what she would say to him, how she would let him know what was happening to her. She wanted him to think this was a good thing, not be hurt that she hadn't felt very much at first.

Charles was in the kitchen, staring into the freezer. "I was thinking of defrosting some chicken," he said when she walked in, without looking at her. "Is that okay for dinner? I thought you could make that cream sauce to go with it."

He was still in his work clothes, his pressed white shirt collar contrasting sharply with his golden-brown skin. He had a mole at the nape of his neck, and Sheila had the urge to kiss it.

Her throat constricted. She couldn't draw enough breath to answer him. They were married, she told herself. They'd had sex dozens of times. It shouldn't feel so difficult to reach for him, to whisper in his ear that she thought she might be able to come if he would only touch her.

She closed the space between them one slow step at a time. Charles shut the freezer door and turned, frowning. "Are you all right?"

Sheila froze and he came to her, his arms circling her body. The heat of him was almost more than she could stand, and she buried her face in his chest. She breathed in the clean, sophisticated scent of his cologne, lemon with balsamic undertones. She didn't know when the shy boy she'd dated in college had become this alluring man, but he was making her shiver.

Charles pulled back, concern creasing his forehead. "Sheila?"

"I—" Her eyes prickled. She tried to hold back, afraid that crying would make her unattractive to him. "I want you," Sheila said in a rush, and the emotion was more than she could restrain. A tear escaped the corner of her eye and rolled down her cheek.

Charles blinked, clearly taken aback. "You want me to what?"

She grabbed for his hand and guided it awkwardly to her side. She knew she should have brought it to a sexier place, but lacked the courage to lewdly direct him to her breast. She squared her shoulders and forced herself to meet his eyes. "I want you. To, um..."

Sheila gave up on speaking, wrapped her arms around his neck, and pulled his mouth down to hers. His surprised moan drowned in the heat of her kiss. She had never been sure what to do with her tongue, and most of their kisses now were close-mouthed. This time, she parted her lips and pressed her tongue forward, into his mouth, and she hoped that her enthusiasm would make up for any lack of finesse.

The shape of his body against hers changed as Charles began to kiss her back. He rubbed his hands up and down her sides at first, still seeming confused, but when Sheila did not pull away, he caught at her lower back and gathered her in close. Settled tightly against him, his chest pressed her breasts flat, his feet tangled with hers and his cock made its presence known against her stomach. It seemed impossibly hot, but for the first time that made sense to Sheila because complementary heat was pooling between her legs.

She fumbled for his shirt buttons. Sex had never seemed like a need before, but this time she thought she couldn't bear another second without feeling his bare skin.

He broke their kiss so he could help her. Together, they dragged his shirt off his chest and began to wrestle with his pants. Sheila held her breath. They had mostly had sex in the dark, and she realized she wasn't sure what he looked like naked. She wanted to see his cock, to touch it with her hand instead of just receiving it.

Before she could get his pants over his hips, however, Charles touched her chin. "Sheila, what's going on? What is this?" He was breathing heavily and his voice was thick.

She tried again to find the words. "Last night, I realized... Tonight, I want..." Sheila blew out a frustrated breath and shook her head. "Please," she said, because it was the only word that was really in her head. It repeated there like a refrain.

Charles seemed about to say something else, but then she managed to remove his pants entirely and wrap her hand around his warm, bare cock. She stroked it lightly, thinking about how it had been inside her, how he had been that connected to her. The idea made her clench and moisten, and Sheila couldn't explain to herself why sex had never affected her so much before.

"I just... I want to kiss it," she told him.

Charles nodded, seeming dazed. Sheila bent at the waist and pressed her mouth to the head of it, affectionately. It was softer against her lips than she expected, so she kissed it again. Only when she straightened did she realize that he might have expected her to drop to her knees and put it in her mouth. She blushed and tried an awkward smile.

He didn't seem disappointed. Instead, he mirrored her gesture, planting an affectionate peck on the crotch of the slacks she'd worn to work.

Sheila jumped at the touch.

"Was that okay?" Charles asked.

She didn't know how to explain that her clit now felt taut, like the head of a drum. He had tried to go down on her a few times, but she had always pushed him away. Now confusing images swirled through her mind—his cock, his tongue, his fingers. Sheila had made herself come once, with a showerhead at a friend's house, but that had been a physical effect of the water pressure. She'd never been sure what to fantasize about, but Charles's body was unlocking those secrets for her.

She stripped quickly, right there in the kitchen, before she could lose her nerve.

"You look beautiful," he whispered. "I like being able to see you."

She glanced up, feeling caught out and vulnerable. His gaze on her was soft and admiring, and she wondered if he saw her differently than he had when they met. Had she changed the way he had?

Charles skimmed his fingers down her throat and over her breastbone. "When did my wife turn into this sexy woman?"

Sheila swallowed, shaken by the way his words echoed what she had been thinking about him. More tears threatened, but he didn't seem to mind, so she clutched his body to hers. His ribs expanded and contracted under her cheek. In a fit of courage, she slid her hands down his back and cupped his ass, amazed at the way the firm muscle filled her palms. "Charles, I don't know how it happened. But something *is* different. You were all I could think about today. I want to feel you." Ducking her head in embarrassment, she rubbed her pelvis against his to underscore the sexual intent of her thoughts.

He gave a sharp exhale. "You can do whatever you want with me."

Remembering what she'd been thinking about over dinner the night before, Sheila said, "I want to sit in your lap and kiss you."

Without hesitation, Charles lifted her and walked them to the nearest chair. His cock was hard under her as she took his face in her hands and kissed and kissed him. She explored his mouth until her jaw ached and her lips were sore, and at some point she realized that her hips had begun to gyrate and that both of them moaned with need. Charles had his hands all over her body—her inner thigh, the back of her head, the base of her spine. Sheila needed more, and now she did catch his fingers and bring them to the space between her legs.

Charles gasped. "I've never felt you this wet."

"I told you," Sheila moaned as he began running his hand up and down her slick slit. "Something is different."

It was as if she'd woken up in someone else's body that morning. She parted her legs for him, and when he slipped a finger inside her, she squeezed it in welcome and began to rock against his hand. It felt better than she could remember having experienced before. Her muscles were tight all over. She thought of Amy and couldn't imagine that any of her visiting lecturers could have felt this delicious.

"Will you let me try something?" Charles asked.

Sheila nodded.

"I think we can make this work right on this chair," he said.

Neither of them quite knew how to maneuver into position, but Sheila had never been so motivated. She eventually turned to face him, her legs thrown over his and her weight braced on his shoulders. She kept her lips on his as much as she could between logistics and frustrated grunts as they found the angle necessary for Charles to guide himself into her.

"Oh god," Charles said. "I can't believe this is happening."

She engulfed his cock with unprecedented ease, and paused for one stunned moment, aware that she was filled to the core with her husband, right there in the middle of the kitchen. She felt herself stretched around him, her nerves still desperate for his touch, her mouth exhausted yet not tired of his kisses.

She tried to move, but the sensation was overwhelming. "I think I'm stuck," Sheila said with an embarrassed giggle.

"That's okay. Stay like that."

She did, knowing that she would have felt silly if she weren't so turned on.

"May I touch you?" Charles asked, and in answer she pulled his hand to the spot where she wanted it most. As soon as he began to stroke her clit, Sheila sobbed with relief and desire. Amy had blistered her ear with sex advice a few times, but Sheila had never understood how good it would feel to have Charles inside her while he worked her with his fingers.

He was a little awkward, too, not always touching her in the exact way she would have liked, but that didn't matter, because she felt slippery and sexy and ready to stay in his lap all night.

She was still kissing him when the sensation began to bubble up from deep within her and her hips began to rock of their own accord. Moving had seemed impossible before, but now it was necessary, and instinct taught her skills she hadn't known she possessed. Charles groaned, his finger stilling. Sheila grabbed his hand and pressed it to her clit so she could grind against it, working until that inner bubble burst and she felt herself get even wetter around his cock.

Charles flung his head back like a man possessed. He seemed to grow inside her, and they were both sweating and gasping. It was like nothing they had done before.

She was almost afraid to meet his eyes after it was over,

when her orgasm had settled into a pleasant ache and she could feel him softening inside her. When she did, however, she was glad, because he was smiling at her with a glowing tenderness that made another tear run down the side of her face. "I want you, too, you know, Sheila," he said. "More and more, it seems like."

She nodded, swallowing hard against a surge of emotion. "That's it," she said. "That's what's different. Everybody talks about how it dies down, but with you it's growing. And what we did tonight—" She shifted, realizing he was still ensconced within her. "I don't think I could have done that at first. I just wasn't ready for something like this until, well, now."

Charles kissed the side of her face. "That doesn't seem like a problem."

Sheila nodded, but before exhilaration could win out, she had to get the last bit off her chest. "I feel kind of stupid," she confessed. "I don't think I understood when we got married. I thought I loved you, but now I'm not sure."

He fixed her with a serious expression. "Do you think you love me now?"

"Yes," she said. "That's why I think I didn't before. It's so strong now."

"Sheila." His fingers down her spine were impossibly tender. "I love you, too—at least I think I do. But wouldn't it be great if five years, ten years, twenty years from now, we're having this same conversation? Saying we couldn't have really loved each other in the past because of how strong it's grown to be?"

Sheila tried and failed to imagine what it would be like to feel even more for her husband than she did at that moment. She thought of all the years she'd believed she wasn't the type to feel passion. "You make it sound pretty good to be a late bloomer," she told him.

Charles hugged her close. "You're not the only one, you know. It's stronger for me, too. Every day, I feel it more."

Sheila hung on to him. She'd fallen for her husband all right, but she was only now realizing how much farther she had to go.

# SUNDAY MORNINGS LIKE THESE

Kiki DeLovely

"I don't know what I'm doing here." I fiddled with the lip-gloss in my pocket, looking around, trying to take in my surroundings. Towering bookcases, threatening to topple from their sheer volume, lined three of the walls. Every inch of the fourth wall was plastered with a mix of art and mirrors, creating quite the unique, massive piece of artwork as a whole. It was a lot to process.

"I think you do." He somehow seemed equally nervous yet worlds more confident, hints of flirtation in his voice.

"Okay, yes, I do. I suppose it's more the why that confounds me. But...I trust you." As I looked up through my eyelashes, his boldness was contagious and my tone dipped into sultry waters.

"You shouldn't," he said candidly, without hesitation, reading past my timbre and into the uncertainty in my eyes—deep chocolate, flecked with shades of amber, honey and doubt. "We've only just met. Don't believe anything I say."

I pondered the advantages of distrust. A value in which I'd always placed my confidence. Did he know how often my previous lovers had deceived me? That I had become a liar in return? I flushed in embarrassment. Our interactions up to this point had been too quickly intimate; we'd been overly generous with ourselves, necessitating a certain degree of faith. My heart trembled at this thought but my breath slowed, creating calm.

"It's too soon," he continued. "But you already knew that too."

Of course. Words had always tricked me. Ever willing to take others at face value, I had believed everything my exes told me. Even when alarms sounded in my gut. Ignoring the queasiness I felt, I simply continued forward, headlong toward imminent disaster and heartache. My last ex—two years gone now—had left me heartbroken and dead broke. An almost risible desperation to see the best in others was my most obvious fault.

The timing was all off. These are not the kinds of words a woman wants to hear before going in for a kiss, but it was fitting with my awkward nature so I just went with it. He cradled my face in his palms like I was the most precious thing in the universe and kissed me like I was the dirtiest.

My lips were eager to keep moving even after I had torn myself away.

"I need to learn to trust myself."

*Shit. Did I just say that out loud?* Staring off somewhere far, far away, I felt a profound realization swiftly coming into focus. I needed to place my confidence in me alone. Trust in what I felt—the steadfastness in my heart, the authenticity I sensed in his touch, the beauty unfurling within me. My intuition was pleading for attention. It already knew how this story would unfold. And once I learned how to believe in myself above all others, the rest would fall into place.

I leaned in again and our kiss deepened, my body pressing into his, his hand snaking around into my hair. He tugged ever so slightly, testing the waters, then reveling in my responsiveness. A moan originated in my mouth, reverberated in his. A kiss so satisfying it felt like making love. And just before we parted, he kissed me so tenderly it felt as if he placed a crystal of light on my tongue. I didn't know it at the time, but the more truth I spoke, the more it sparkled and shone its light into the world, spreading magic that glimmered to far reaches, illuming every corner. We spent the rest of the night in his bed, surprisingly clothed, sharing bits of our pasts in between passionate spells of making out. The more I opened up to him, the more the crystal sparked and tingled and spoke my truth, jogging hidden depths of myself, unearthing long-forgotten secrets and bringing them to light. Secrets cemented so securely that I had mistaken them for truth all these years, blindly accepting them as fact and simply building upon them.

The crystal tasted like refracted light after a long rain. His kisses tasted like coming home.

Somewhere around four a.m. we had found ourselves in his kitchen, making hot chocolate and eating whatever we could find that didn't take much effort. We couldn't keep our hands off each other long enough to actually cook something and I, for one, certainly couldn't be trusted with a knife.

"Um. Who the hell keeps dragon fruit stocked in their kitchen?" I couldn't help teasing him as I palmed the scaly beast, secretly impressed.

"You know what the heck that thing is?"

Once the giggling fit began, it felt uncontainable. Clearly both giddy and more than a little slap-happy from lack of sleep, I couldn't do anything but nod my head several times in response, my eyes squeezing shut against the tears of delight.

"I force myself to try something new every time I go grocery shopping," he explained. Obviously I was going to need a moment. "This time I couldn't resist the pink allure of this beauty." Catching the slightest hint of innuendo in his voice sobered me quickly and I decided to play along with my own insinuations.

"Well, it's deliciously ripe. The perfect amount of firmness with just enough give. You chose well." I tossed it to him, enjoying that I got to be the authority on the matter at hand. "Slice it in half, lengthwise."

"Oh, wow! I certainly wasn't expecting that!" He marveled at its shockingly white flesh speckled with black seeds.

"Gorgeous, huh?"

He didn't respond, instead fixing on me a look that willingly betrayed the unspoken in his mind. I, in turn, nervously sought out a spoon, handing it to him with a shy smile.

Reassuming instructor mode, I continued, "You can scoop it out bite by bite, if you like, or the entire thing at once..."

"I like to take my time."'

Again met with that unnerving gaze, I was determined not to let it shake me. "But you have to be careful not to slice into the pink skin. Tempting as it might be, it's inedible."

"I'm always careful with the pink bits." The line was so cheesy that had the sexual tension between us not been so all consuming, I probably would've laughed in his face. But his expression was so piercing he could've primed me with any ridiculous line and it wouldn't have mattered. This time I didn't look away, taking in the possibilities dazzling in his eyes. Having already known the wonders of his talented tongue, I couldn't resist fantasizing further.

He spoon-fed me a bite and ran his mouth down my neck. I was delectably pinned between him and the countertop.

"Mmm… I want more."

"More fruit or more of me?" His taunts were the perfect mix of playfulness and prurience.

"Yes, please."

Obligingly, he pulled my dress off over my head before scooping another spoonful of seedy flesh into my mouth and making his way down my body. He quickly veered away from the ticklish sides of my waist and continued kissing across the curve of my belly, nuzzling against my panties, inhaling my scent, mouthing me through the silk. His fervency canceled out any lingering bits of shyness I may have had at that point and I wrestled with that remaining piece of fabric as though my life depended on it. I suppose in that moment it did. Looking up at me with those eyes, he gave my panties one final commanding tug before diving in.

"Oh, fffffuck…"

Any intelligible speech had abandoned me as I descended farther and farther into nonverbal groans and grunts. His tongue, quite nicely occupied, met me in that regard—the moans from the back of his throat vibrating into the depths of my pussy, heightening my pleasure all the more. He read my desire like a picture book and continued moaning superfluously simply because he loved how wild it drove me. My body shuddering against him, neck arched, hands hysterically grasping and clawing at whatever was within reach. His flesh or mine—or even that of a fruit—proved too tempting for my fingers to resist. I'm pretty sure at one point we were both wearing dragon fruit pulp after the poor creature met its untimely demise in my clutches.

Goodness, he wasn't kidding about taking his time. I couldn't help but wonder at one point whether his knees or tongue would be the first to give out. But neither did. He kept at it until I had come in his mouth twice, eating me out like he was starving and

I was the last meal on earth. The feel of his eager mouth sucking my clit, that tongue of his fucking my hole, teeth gently biting and tugging on my lips, not to mention the moans working vibrational magic—it was easily the best head of my life.

And then he started in with his fingers. It was around that time that my legs finally gave out and I joined him on the linoleum. He worked two and then three fingers into my cunt, fucking me so slowly I thought I might cry. Forcing me to feel every millimeter from his fingertips up to his knuckles, sliding in and out of me so sweetly, causing me to emit new little sounds each time his thumb pressed firmly up against my clit. Then, without the slightest bit of warning, as if he were hit by a bolt of lightning, his thrusts took off at a feverish pace, my voice crying out unearthly noises and my body spasming in sensory overload. Before I knew it, his fingers were curling up, stroking my G-spot, and I was shooting all over the place. I shrieked one final time, a long, hot stream raining down on both of us.

"Mmm...it's been a long time since I've been with a woman who could squirt. I was hoping..." His sentence drifted off as he marveled at dreams become reality soaking into his jeans. Come not his own dripping down his pant leg. Yes, it had been much too long. For both of us. I was beside myself—not wanting to move an inch—my naked body glistening with all kinds of juices juxtaposed with his clothed self. I lay there unabashedly blissed out, not having known it was possible to lose oneself so entirely in desire like that. Going there with him was just another way in which I embraced more of myself, shimmering in my truth.

And so it was that cracks began to form in my deep-seated fear of vulnerability, innocent beams of light peeking through the foundation at first, gradually forming hairline fractures that would soon enough break open, leveling the entire structure. I won't lie—not anymore, at least—this looming demolition scared me shitless. If it had not been for a swiftly mounting safe haven that enveloped me in its place, I might have been tempted to run.

That was six months ago. And now I'm beyond grateful for having stayed. Especially on Sunday mornings like these. When the sunlight has already been creeping in for hours and the sex is still exploratory. Tracing his fingers over my hips—a physical continuation of his visual admiration—I'm spellbound under his regard. His eyes take in all of me; his hands take all they can. I feel seen, unabashedly beautiful with every sweep of his fingertips across my skin, his gaze going deeper still. Each slow moment more crushingly intimate and blush-worthy than the next.

But that's just the tender buildup. I'm the type of gal who doesn't need much, if any, foreplay. Which is exactly what makes his leisurely pace all the more excruciating. He's slow. Likes to tease out every last drop of anticipation, driving me to the edge and back again. And then, just after the point where I think I'm going to lose it, he's flipping me over, taking me from behind with a frenzied rhythm.

Leading by example, his presence at my side has proven to be an easy comfort. A bewitching inspiration guiding me toward a life built on honesty and openness. He breathes new life into me, new light into my being. And I, in turn, seem to spark an opening up in him.

"I think maybe..." he begins hesitantly, looking up at me with eyes rich and dark like a bold French roast, unsure how to go about asking for a desire that was only just now awakening in him. "I'm kind of curious..." He stops himself again until finally it all tumbles out quite quickly. "I want you to choke me."

I hold his gaze steadily, my eyes dancing in delight, making sure that he knows how much his request turns me on. I feel honored that he's willing to entrust me with it. The thick layer of his vulnerability apparent in bringing up a budding hunger. Luckily it's not new for me, so I feel confident indulging his latest yearning, given a few caveats. Sexual adventurousness and spontaneity may be qualities we both value highly in each other but safety always comes first, especially when our perverse proclivities involve great risk.

We discuss both the pleasures and hazards of breath play, safetaps (the nonverbal equivalent of safewords), and I share my extensive knowledge on the subject, making it clear that complete asphyxiation is off the table. It's simply too dangerous. This is one kink I don't play around with lightly.

Once I feel reassured that we've lessened the risks as much as possible and he knows exactly what he's getting himself into, we waste no time in getting to work. While shimmying out of every last bit of clothing, we roll around in bed, making out and rubbing up against each other. I push him down on his back, sucking on his tongue one last time before backing off. The veins in his neck throb with lust and anticipation.

"Stroke yourself for me." I watch appreciatively as he gets more and more excited, wrapping my hand around his neck, resting it there lightly. His cock shoots straight up from the mere suggestiveness of my palm's presence.

I can tell this is going to be quick and dirty, so I climb on top, my pussy swallowing his cock whole in one fluid motion. He groans and I tighten my grasp slightly, careful not to put pressure on the windpipe, getting wetter as the tension builds between us. This is getting me just as hot as it is getting him hard. His hips buck recklessly under me and I force myself to focus. I let up briefly, allowing his blood flow and breath to regulate. Then I go back in again, a little more forcefully this time, ever cautious with the amount of pressure and mindful of how many seconds have passed. With his eyes wide, I stare back intently, observing the mingling of panic and lust, our bond solidified all the more as we wade into intense emotional depths. Our physical pleasures melding with an entirely new level of spirituality. I catch myself holding my own breath.

Our voracity mounts, me delighting in the rasp of his breathing, he reveling in newfound sensations. Sensing that he's close to the edge, I go in for a long, deep kiss at just the right moment. My pussy squeezing his cock as my hand tightens around his throat. His orgasm pounds powerfully out of him and into me. A full spectrum of colors flash behind my eyelids as I come, riding him through every last wave.

We've come a long way since that first night in his apartment when he told me not to place my confidence in his words. Our little piece of magic brings about change—expanding my world in ways unimaginable, gently spreading into the world at large. From the get-go, we could both sense the limitlessness of it all around us. Humanity was becoming somehow more humane. The Earth an infinitely more habitable place. And it starts so simply. Sunday mornings like these. The sheets crumpled around us, his ethereal body intertwined with mine as we lie side by side. We inhale each other, exhaling prisms of light into the universe, murmurs of love and adoration on our breath.

# LOTUS

## Emerald

It was time for a brand-new one. Though Charlotte loved all stages of her favorite hobby, breaking out an unopened box and turning it upside down over the table held an undeniable special rush. As the thousand carved cardboard pieces heaped onto the wood surface, she stood the box up to her left and began to spread out and flip them so they were all shiny-side-up.

Charlotte's gaze surveyed the jumble of what looked like chaos in front of her, a part of her psyche already resting with the confidence of seeing the order. It hadn't manifested yet, but that part of her knew it was there. She had developed a sense of perception around the details in a puzzle's picture that afforded her a solid assurance that however challenging a puzzle seemed—and they were all challenging in their own way—the pieces of any one could always be put together. It was one of the things she loved most about puzzles: they could always be mastered.

As she finished flipping the pieces, Charlotte scoured the table, seeking the straight edges among the myriad curves and angles. In the years she'd been doing them, puzzles had developed into almost a companion in her life, a steadfast focus that was always renewable. She started and finished puzzles the way some people started and finished reading books. She had even been known to time things according to them. It had been almost exactly a year ago, for instance, that she'd made the internal agreement that she would move out of Ralph's apartment when she finished the eight-hundred-piece farm scene. Ralph had worked on it alongside her sometimes, Charlotte's stomach continually clenching with the secret knowledge of what their progress meant as they pieced together the faded red barn with horses grazing in the foreground.

At the time, the impending action had felt excruciating; now it was like a passing breeze, a memory that made her glance up for just a second before focusing again on the fresh underwater scene in front of her.

Charlotte's cell phone rang as she caught sight of the first corner amongst the mass of cardboard. Not recognizing the number, she debated whether or not to answer as she spotted a second corner. Sliding it toward her with one finger, she picked up and answered the phone with her other hand.

"Hello?"

"Hi, this is Gavin Shannon, calling in response to your email inquiry on my website." The voice was smooth and professional, and Charlotte instantly recognized the name of the photographer whose site she had encountered the day before.

"Oh, yes, hi," she said. "Thanks for calling back."

"Of course. I am available to do a shoot at the botanical gardens you mentioned, and I'd be happy to set up a time."

"Oh, great." Charlotte pulled the third corner toward her and moved a few edge pieces to their appropriate side before realizing she wasn't paying attention to the voice in her ear that was now talking about rates and scheduling.

"Tomorrow?" she asked, catching the word as she sat back and did her best to shift her attention. "Yes, I could do that. I have no idea how long this might take or anything like that. There's just a particular thing I'd like a photo of, and I don't take pictures well enough to do it justice."

Gavin laughed warmly. "Something tells me you may underrate yourself," he said, his voice light, "but again, I'm more than happy to help you out."

For some reason Charlotte almost felt herself blush. It was a charming compliment, and despite his knowing nothing about her, he had somehow managed to make it sound sincere.

Charlotte said good-bye and set the phone beside her on the table. Though she loved the idea of personalized puzzles, she had only had them made of two of her own photographs. One was a close-up of a pale-pink peony bush, in full majestic bloom outside her grandparent's house several years ago. The framed puzzle had hung in their dining room until they'd both passed away. Then it had reverted to her, and it hung now above her fireplace.

The other was of her beloved cocker spaniel, Lucky, who'd died two years before at the age of sixteen. The framed portrait of him she'd painstakingly put together—it had, somehow, worked like a slow channeler of her grief, though she hadn't been able to even touch it until more than a month after his death—was on the wall above her bed. She still remembered the moment she'd captured the image. Lucky had rolled onto his back, his madly wagging tail blurry as it wiggled like a snake along the ground. To this day, Charlotte's heart lurched a tiny bit every time she caught sight of the framed puzzle that was easily the most meaningful one she had ever put together.

Still, Charlotte knew she was no photographer. It didn't seem that hard—just aim the camera at what she wanted a photo of and push the button—but her very lack of success in deriving the desired outcome from doing just that indicated how much more there was to photography than she understood. It was a skill she admired greatly.

The lotus puzzle was something she wanted to do for Connie. Perhaps it would lift her spirits. If not, Charlotte hoped that at the very least it would help her feel supported. Connie hadn't been very far along when the miscarriage had happened, and Charlotte knew it wasn't as heart wrenching as it could have been. But she knew too that it had been a very wanted child, and Connie's pain had been evident enough when Charlotte had gone to see her best friend when she'd gotten the call last week.

The pond at the local botanical gardens was one of Connie's favorite things, and Charlotte had seen the lone pink lotus flower a couple of days before during a solitary visit. She'd snapped her own picture with her cell phone camera, but it hadn't nearly done justice to the splendor of the blossom as it graced its lily pad with a kind of transcendence. Charlotte didn't even own a "real" camera and realized that for what she wanted to do, it would be best to hire a professional.

Despite her eagerness only moments before, Charlotte felt a bit restless now as she looked down at the pieces in front of her. Pushing aside the notion that the phone conversation she'd just had was responsible for the inexplicable butterflies, Charlotte pushed back from the table and headed for the stairs, deciding to indulge in her second-favorite pastime before getting back to the new puzzle. She grabbed a towel, passed through the bedroom and reached for the tap of her beloved oversized bathtub.

* * *

When she emerged from her car the following day, Charlotte caught sight of a figure crossing the parking lot from the other side. Squinting, she made out a black camera bag slung over the man's shoulder and stopped to wait on the sidewalk.

As he drew closer, Charlotte's stomach dropped a little. Even with a winter coat on, Gavin's figure evidenced a solid build, muscular but graceful. His dark hair framed classic features arranged in a friendly, open expression as he approached. He smiled when he caught her eye.

"Hi. You must be Charlotte? I'm Gavin."

He extended his hand, and Charlotte took it automatically, trying to find her tongue.

"Of course. It's a pleasure to meet you," she finally managed, trying to calm the fluttering in her stomach as they headed toward the door. Gavin held it for her, and Charlotte ducked out of the bitter wind into the slight shock of the hot, humid atmosphere of the greenhouse.

"This heat feels great for about three seconds, then it gets a little overwhelming to the other extreme," Charlotte said with a breathless laugh as they hung their coats on the rack inside the door.

Gavin smiled. "I'm sure I can handle it. I'm from San Antonio originally."

"Really? You don't have much of an accent."

He chuckled. "I went to college in Minneapolis, and it eventually went away for the most part. You may still catch me calling you 'ma'am' on occasion, though." He winked at her.

Charlotte smiled and led the way to the pond, biting her lip as she caught a whiff of his aftershave. "Did you go to school for photography?"

"Yep. I minored in business, though, in case I needed

something to fall back on." He laughed as they neared the water. "Is this the pond?"

"Yes. There's a lotus blooming in the middle of it, and I want a picture of it to make into a puzzle."

"Really? What a cool idea. Sounds like extra work though... why don't you just have it blown up and frame it?"

"I love doing puzzles," Charlotte answered, feeling a bit felt self-conscious. It sounded a little silly put like that. "This one is for a friend, actually. She loves this place. I think it'll just give it more of a...personal touch. She and her husband went through a challenge recently, and I want to do this to support her."

Gavin glanced at her. "That's awesome," he said as she stopped in front of the water. "Beautiful," he murmured, peering over the short stone wall separating it from the path as his hands went to his camera.

"Yes," she agreed. "I'm not sure if I want something relatively close-up with just a few of the lily pads around it, or one that's farther back so she can identify the pond...."

"I'll take some of both," Gavin said, already starting to aim and click a few feet away from her. Charlotte sensed a shift in him as he began to work. His attention went fully to the contraption in his hands, the eye nearest her squeezed shut as he varied the camera's angle and snapped several pictures in a row.

"It's so amazing to see things like this blooming in here when it's literally freezing outside," Charlotte said after a while.

Gavin was walking back and forth along the path in a kind of almost dance, repositioning his tripod and snapping pictures from different angles. "Yeah. Some lotus species can survive colder temperatures, though not as cold as it is here. They can keep themselves in bloom down to about fifty degrees, though."

"Really?"

"Yeah. They're able to regulate their temperature to some degree—no pun intended. They can heat their own blossoms when it's colder out to attract the pollinators they need to reproduce."

Charlotte stared at him. "I had no idea plants could do that sort of thing."

Gavin shrugged as he adjusted the tripod, pointing the camera toward the pond and clicking away. "I think we underestimate a lot about plants. How they fit into the whole ecosystem thing. My sister's a master gardener at one of the park systems in Maryland. I probably know more about plants than the average person from hearing to her talk about them." He pushed the shutter one last time and straightened to face her. "Any other angles you want me to hit?"

The question made her cheeks tinge pink for some reason, and she shook her head.

"So won't it take you a while to put the puzzle together?" Gavin asked as they walked back to the exit.

Charlotte shrugged. "Depends on what you mean by 'a while.'"

Gavin snorted. "I think it took me about a year to finish the last jigsaw puzzle I did. That was probably sometime when I was teenager, maybe even younger." He gave her a crooked smile that seemed a bit self-deprecating. She remembered her own self-consciousness and felt strangely touched that he appeared to care how she might see that.

"I think it's like a lot of things in that the more you do it, the better—or in this case, faster—you get at it."

She was finding Gavin easier to talk to than anyone she'd met in a while. When they reached the coatrack, he hurried to grab her coat and helped her into it. Charlotte caught her breath as his hand brushed hers. She slipped her arms quickly into the sleeves.

"Thank you. That's very Southern-gentlemanly of you," she teased.

She thought she saw Gavin blush himself then, but he turned and reached for his own coat before she could tell for sure. They took a moment to bundle up, and Gavin held the door open as Charlotte stepped back out into winter, the biting cold surrounding them as the glass swung shut behind them.

Two days later Charlotte left work early, wanting to get home before the foot of snow predicted for the evening started to fall. Visual evidence of the previous night's ice storm still covered the non-road surfaces as she entered her neighborhood. Crystalline shards of fallen ice littered the ground beneath larger trees, and the bushes lining the road to her house looked as though they had aged overnight and sprouted identical heads of icy white hair.

Charlotte wasted no time drawing a hot bath when she arrived home.

Sighing contentedly, she sank into the liquid heat and looked up at the large windows that framed the corner tub. The temperature difference inside and out was drastic enough that the glass had steamed up, but she could still make out the first of the snow starting to fall beyond it. As she watched the flakes grow thicker, Charlotte pictured the lotus bloom, delicate and protected from the scathing winter temperatures inside its giant glass dome. An image of the photographer who had last accompanied her to see it followed, and she shivered a little despite the warmth surrounding her.

The phone on the tile ledge beside her rang, and she turned her head to check the number. The low buzz in her stomach grew stronger.

Pushing herself up, she quickly towel-dried her hair and leaned on the edge of the tub to answer. "Hello?"

"Hi, it's Gavin. I hope you're staying warm in this latest imminent blizzard of ours."

Charlotte's breath caught. "I am warm indeed," she said, noting that his tone of voice would almost certainly have done the trick even if she hadn't been submerged in heated water.

Gavin chuckled. "Well, I'm calling because I have your proofs here and wanted to see if you wanted to come by the studio on your way home to take a look at them."

Charlotte felt a stab of disappointment as she explained that she was already home for the day due to the forecast. "I'm terrible at driving in snow," she said with a self-conscious laugh.

"I understand." Gavin paused. "I'd be happy to come to you if you'd like. I can close up here any time and bring them by your place."

The butterflies in Charlotte's belly jumped in unison.

"Okay," she said, managing to keep her cool. "Of course, that means you'll have to drive more in the snow yourself—and you might even get stuck here." She bit her lip, realizing she could think of worse things than having to host Gavin for the night.

"True," he said casually. "But my truck is four-wheel-drive, and I got pretty used to driving in the snow when I lived in Minnesota. If you're worried about it, though, we can wait a day or two." Gavin sounded like he was smiling.

"No, that's okay," Charlotte said, smiling too. She gave him her address and hung up the phone, then carefully set it back on the ledge before climbing out of the tub.

Downstairs, she ran her eyes around the living room. Her "puzzle table," as she called it, was the centerpiece of one-half of room, with the other half devoted to a couch and love seat facing each other perpendicular to the brick fireplace. She had forgone a coffee table in favor of end tables flanking each piece, preferring the open space in front of the fireplace that was covered with her grandparents' antique rug. She flipped a switch on the wall, and a small burst of flames materialized behind the fireplace's glass.

As a potential preparation occurred to her, Charlotte bit her lip, wondering if she was being overambitious. Finally she rolled her eyes and dashed from the room, returning with two condoms that she slipped into the small drawer in the end table closest to her. Her cheeks burned as she told herself she was probably hugely misreading Gavin's intentions in coming there. Still, might as well be on the safe side.

The doorbell rang, and Gavin smiled at her as he stepped inside. His eyes swept over the room, and he smiled wider when he saw the puzzle table.

"Do you always have one in progress?" he asked, walking over to look at the partially finished underwater scene.

"Usually," she answered. "May I take your coat?"

Gavin shrugged out of it, revealing a smart black button-down shirt over jeans, which he filled out ridiculously well. Charlotte turned and carried his coat to the closet, willing the blush she could feel in her cheeks to subside.

"I wouldn't even know where to start," Gavin murmured as she retuned to the table, his eyes running over the pieces. "How do you even begin to put this thing together?"

"Well, first you find the four corners. Then you look for the edges and work on the border until it's done. I then sort the pieces according to approximately where they go, which I haven't really gotten to on this one.

"The thing is, there's a way to look at every piece and then study the total picture and match at least one particular detail—thus figuring out where the piece goes. Even if no pieces are yet together in the vicinity, I can usually look at one and find a detail on it that matches the picture and place it at least in the area where it will eventually go.

"Take this piece," she said, picking up one that was a combination of turquoise and a textured-looking red.

She studied the picture for several moments. Gavin didn't say anything, but she sensed him watching closely. Eventually she found it. "So it goes up in this area," she said, placing the piece in an empty spot inside the puzzle's border. Picking up the box, she pointed at the picture. "It's an edge of the red starfish with water behind it. See the way the angle in the piece matches the one in the picture right there, and the little bumps on the starfish are arranged the same way?"

"That's quite an eye for detail."

Charlotte set the box down. "Well, you must have that kind of perception too, right, as a photographer?"

Gavin looked thoughtful. "I'm not sure it's the same. I think I see whole pictures rather than details. I don't usually see something and identify all the little things about it that make it up. I just look at something and know I like what I see." Charlotte felt a tingle rush through her as his eyes flicked almost imperceptibly up and down her. "And usually that's when I start taking pictures."

"I guess that makes sense," Charlotte said. "After all, I can put a puzzle together but don't know the first thing about taking a decent picture." She laughed and glanced at the peony puzzle hanging above the fireplace.

Gavin followed her gaze.

"I took that one," she said a bit nervously before he could ask. "That's one of only two puzzles I've had made out of photos of my own."

"Now, see, that's a beautiful shot," Gavin drawled, a touch of Southern accent tingeing his voice as he stepped closer to the frame. He pushed his hands into his pockets as he gazed up at it, and Charlotte bit her lip as she studied his form from behind.

"Would you like to sit down?" She gestured at the furniture and fidgeted internally, not sure whether to initiate sitting on the love seat or stay with the safety of the couch. She decided to let him choose and hung back.

Gavin hesitated, then headed for the couch. He sat somewhat near the middle of it, and Charlotte sat on one side, not quite up against the arm but not on top of him, either.

"I hope you find something that works in these," he said as he pulled a batch of prints out of his bag.

"I'm sure I will." Without meaning to, Charlotte drifted closer to him as she looked at the first print over his shoulder.

Her lips parted as she took in the electrifying hues of one of the most pristine images she'd ever seen. Layers of emerald lily pads reached to each edge of the photo and glistened like they were lacquered, offering a backdrop for the graceful cluster of petals that rose like a velvet fire in nuanced shades of pink she hadn't begun to notice when she'd looked at it in person. Every surface seemed to rise off the page like it was close enough to be touched; the water droplets on the leaves looked as though they might burst any second.

"Oh," she breathed, taking the photo from him. After a few moments, she accepted the next print he handed her. This one, too, was stunning, depicting the lotus bloom from the other side, with a bit of the pond visible in one corner and a more prominent view of the fringed yellow seedpod.

Gavin handed her a third one. It was one of the distance shots, the frame encompassing the surrounding water and foliage that bordered the pond. The lotus itself was just off-center, complemented by a background of tall yellow flowers that laced the far end of the pond, draping green branches from the small tree that hovered over the water to the right and jagged rock wall that extended around the pond to the left. The lotus sat alone, like a beacon in a sea of shiny green splendor.

Charlotte looked at the picture for a long time, knowing the location would be instantly recognizable to Connie. "These are amazing," she said finally, tearing her eyes from the photo to look up at him.

She caught a look in his eyes she wasn't sure she was supposed to see. Gavin was watching her deeply, intensely, hungrily. Though she worried she'd caught him doing something he didn't want her to, he didn't look away, but rather cleared his throat and smiled as he sat back against the cushions.

"I'm so glad you think so. It was beautiful subject matter, of course. You have good taste."

His eyes, Charlotte thought, still looked hungry. Flustered, she glanced away and said, "Can I get you something to drink?"

"Sure." Gavin got up and followed her to the kitchen as she started listing what she had in the fridge. As she reached it, her gaze flicked to the window, and she paused.

"Snow's really coming down," she said, a note of concern in her voice as she watched the flurry of white on the other side of the glass. "I hope you'll be able to get out okay. I'll feel really bad if you get stuck here." She turned back to him, realizing the words weren't altogether true.

Gavin laughed, glancing behind her out the window. "I can think of worse things," he said lightly.

Charlotte felt as though her breath was lightly pulled out from underneath her as he met her eyes again, the combination of hunger and restraint more subtle now but still there. Flustered, she gestured behind her to the refrigerator.

"So, what would you like?"

Gavin was standing a few feet away, but he moved slowly

toward her as she watched him. Giving her plenty of time to move had she wanted to, he finally said in a low voice, "You."

The moment froze. Then he was kissing her, pressing her back against the counter as his body pushed into hers. Charlotte's breath vanished, and heat shot straight from her belly to her cunt as Gavin reached his arms around her and pulled her somehow closer. A tiny moan spilled from her throat as she ground against him, and she found herself willing their clothes to simply disappear.

Gavin stepped back just far enough to lift her off her feet, and seconds later he was lowering her back onto the couch in the living room. Charlotte arched her back as he climbed on top of her, his movements somehow urgent and measured at the same time.

She ground herself against him, and Gavin groaned as he rose to his knees, almost ripping the buttons on his shirt in his haste to get them undone. Charlotte sat up and pulled off her sweater, falling back to the cushions as she dropped it on the rug beside them.

Gavin breathed heavily as his eyes ran over her body. The carnal lust in them made Charlotte greedy for his touch, and she grabbed his hands, pressing one to her breast and pulling the other to her mouth. She ran her tongue over his fingertips, and Gavin's breath hissed when she pulled one into her mouth, sucking hungrily as he reached beneath her and unsnapped her bra. Pulling it off roughly, he leaned down and latched his teeth over a nipple, making her cry out.

Charlotte reached down and ran a strong hand over Gavin's denim-covered erection, and he pulled back to wrench his pants open. When he jumped up to pull them off, Charlotte stared at the diamond-hard cock in front of her, unable to stop herself from rising to her knees and taking it into her mouth. She sucked it like she had his finger, and Gavin moaned, clenching his fists at his sides. In a moment she felt his hand against her head, not pushing but rather pulling her hair gently away from him.

"You'll make me come," he whispered, panting as he looked down at her. "And I want to be inside you for that."

Charlotte rose up so she was at eye level with him, on her knees on the couch as he stood beside it. She held his gaze for a beat, then stretched over to the small drawer in the end table. Returning to her previous position, she pressed a small package into Gavin's hand and said quietly, "Fuck me, then."

Gavin pushed her back down on the couch, tearing open the wrapper and sliding the condom on in one frantic motion as he knelt between her legs and pulled her into position by her thighs. Charlotte felt the moisture between them as she lifted her hips, willing him to plunge inside her before another second passed.

He complied. She cried out as he entered her, and though she still sensed the restraint in his hard muscles as she gripped his arms, it seemed he soon couldn't help himself and began fucking her with abandon as she squealed uncontrollably. Words came out of her mouth that surprised her, encouraging him to pound her wet cunt and make her take his hard cock and fuck her harder, faster, deeper. She would have been blushing if she hadn't been so consumed by things far more important than decorum.

Suddenly reigning himself in, Gavin pulled back and knelt above her. She could feel his hardness pulsing inside her as he pressed her clit with his thumb. She came almost instantly with an unabashed scream, and Gavin rocked his hips forward and pumped into her for only seconds before he followed suit, groaning her name as he emptied himself inside her.

When he pulled out, Gavin met her eyes and gently leaned down to kiss her, adjusting himself on the couch so their bodies fit side by side. She felt his breath against her hair as the air cooled around them. After a moment, Charlotte's soft voice broke the silence.

"I think you'd better stay here tonight no matter what the weather does."

She felt him smile, the words warm against her skin as he murmured into her shoulder.

"I think you're right."

Charlotte carried the silver eight-by-ten-inch frame into the bathroom and set it on the ledge along the tub. Lifting the hammer, she pounded the picture hanger into the wall across from the windows, then retrieved and carefully hung the brilliant close-up of the shimmering lotus blossom.

She had already placed an order for the exquisite distance shot to be made into the puzzle for Connie. This photo, however, would remain in one piece, its dazzling hues and piercing details a perpetual witness to her cherished time in the tub—starting with tonight. Charlotte felt the heat of anticipation as she leaned down and turned on the tap, testing the temperature for a few seconds before twisting the stopper into place.

As she straightened, the doorbell rang. Charlotte dried her hands and ran downstairs to let Gavin in.

# WHAT HAPPENS AT SEA

Tina Simmons

Three friends on a late summer cruise. It had seemed like the ideal vacation. Keyword: seemed. Sandwiched between the wall and Laura, I swore I would never go on another cruise no matter how much my friends pleaded. I sighed and shifted for the hundredth time, trying to get comfortable on the thin mattress. Between Laura's flailing limbs and the snoring coming from Gina in the bunk above us, I knew I was never going to get to sleep.

With the moves of a contortionist, I managed to crawl out of the bunk without waking Laura or Gina. Taking my pillow and a blanket with me, I left the small, claustrophobic cabin and made my way down the ship's narrow corridors, hoping I wouldn't get lost and wander into some crew member's quarters. I kept a steadying hand on the wall as I went to counter the ship's gentle rocking motions. I could hear a couple arguing behind one door and though their voices were muffled, I could make out almost every word. Something about him not wanting to get married and her being in love with someone else. I shook my head and kept walking, grateful that I at least liked my bunkmates even if I didn't want to sleep in the same space with them, and finally located the ladder to the upper deck. I carefully climbed the narrow rungs, not wanting to add a concussion to my list of complaints about this vacation.

My aggravation at my friends and the weariness of tossing and turning for three hours fled as soon as I stepped on deck. It wasn't one of the big cruise ships that served eight meals a day and had nightly entertainment on three different stages. It was a sailboat cruise, bare bones—which had seemed like an adventure while reading the brochure and now felt a bit too rough for my tastes—with only forty people on board, including the crew. Laura had planned the cruise, convincing Gina and me that it would be more exciting than a traditional cruise because we would get to go to places the regular cruise ships couldn't go. It was supposed to be one last adventure for the three of us before Gina got married in June and Laura went back to grad school in the fall. Instead of a weeklong exotic adventure, it was turning out to be an insomnia-inducing nightmare for me and it was only day two.

The captain had told us we were welcome to sleep on the deck if we liked the idea of camping at sea. He'd pointed out the big foam mats rolled up against the railing and now I unrolled one and threw my pillow down on it. I wasn't much of a camper any more than I was a sailor, but I figured I would probably get more sleep out here—as long as it didn't rain—than I would in the cramped cabin. Lying down on the mat, I stared up at the night sky and felt my breath catch in my throat. We were out to sea now, anchored somewhere in the Caribbean, and the sky was an inky black void dotted with a million sparkling stars. For the first time in two days, I felt at peace. Restful. As if I could fall asleep at any moment.

"Beautiful, isn't it?"

I squeaked and bolted upright. The dangers of city living were too deeply ingrained in me for the sound of an unexpected male voice to not be startling. There was just enough light to make out the flash of white teeth as he smiled.

"Sorry, didn't mean to scare you. Jeremy Fleming, we met yesterday."

Ah yes, Jeremy. He was here alone, a scientist—no, marine biologist—off on a solo holiday. It wasn't unusual for people to travel solo, but men like Jeremy… I let my thoughts trail off, realizing I was peering at him in the darkness.

"Hey. I thought I was alone."

He gave an easy shrug, settling on the wood deck next to my mat. "Sorry. I needed some fresh air." A self-deprecating laugh was followed by another shrug. "Don't tell anyone, but I get a little seasick below decks."

"Ironic," I said, though I found something charming in his confession of vulnerability.

"You, too?"

"No, I don't get seasick, I get cabin-mate sick," I said. "Love my friends, but I can't sleep with them."

He nodded. "Don't sleep with your friends, got it."

I laughed at his solemn tone as I stretched out on my mat again. "Something like that."

"Well, we're not friends," he said, "so can I sleep with you?"

Oh, I wanted to come back with some sharp retort. But I was just too damned tired. "Get your own mat, buddy," I tough-talked, jerking my thumb toward the railing. "And if you snore, I'm tossing you overboard."

He made some crack about being in his element in the ocean or something, but the lull of the rocking ship and the sound of the ocean had done its work. I was asleep before he'd even spread out his mat.

I woke up to glaring sunshine, and the blaring captain giving orders to the crew. After a moment of disorientation, I realized where I was and that I was looking pretty rough in my sleep T-shirt and ragged running shorts. I rolled my mat, gathered my belongings and bolted for the ladder, nearly running smack-dab into Jeremy, who was coming at me with a smile.

"Oh, hey, you're up."

"Uh, yeah, good morning," I said, brushing past him, head low.

"Same time tonight? You and me, we'll sleep together?"

"Sure, uh-huh," I said, waving him off as I headed for my cabin. "No! Wait! What?"

He looked too damned good this early in the morning and it was scrambling my brains. He'd showered; I could smell his shampoo, and his dark hair had that tousled, just-laid look. It was distracting.

He laughed. "Sorry, bad joke by the light of day, I guess."

The ship rolled with the strength of a wave and I lost my balance, bumping against him hard enough that he put his arms up to steady us both. If it had been a movie, it would've been the first-kiss scene. But this wasn't a movie and I was feeling like a grungy ship rat. I braced my hand against the wall and pushed off from his chest, not before noticing that he definitely was built for comfort. Broad chested, strong armed—was this what all marine biologists were like? I never wanted to take another cruise, but it made moving to a coastal city pretty appealing.

"Oh, I got it," I said, somewhat belatedly. I'd put some distance between us, but I suspected I was looking at him like a spider looks at a fly. "Sorry, mornings aren't my best time."

"When are you at your best?"

"At night." As soon as I said it, I realized how it sounded. "I mean, I'm a night owl, usually, and pretty sharp."

He nodded, solemn-faced. "Usually."

He was charming me, to be sure. Who knows how the conversation would've gone if Gina and Laura hadn't bopped into the hall passage. "There you are," Gina said. "We were going to start searching for you."

"She's safe," Jeremy answered for me. "I promise."

I made quick introductions, the girls headed topside and Jeremy meandered off to the galley with a wink and a promise to find me that night. I watched him go, wondering exactly what he meant, but not at all wondering what I wanted it to mean.

After a day of swimming in a bay on Saint Thomas and sightseeing on the island, I had to convince Gina and Laura that I genuinely wanted to sleep on the deck that night, then I had to convince them I wanted to sleep alone. It didn't take them long to catch on.

"Just what happened with you and Mr. Hottie?" Laura asked, as I gathered my blanket and pillow for a second night topside. This time, I was wearing a better-fitting T-shirt and leggings, though I knew it wouldn't much matter in the darkness.

"Nothing," I muttered. "Yet."

He wasn't there when I got up on the deck, but the captain was. We made small talk for a few minutes before he headed off to his cabin and I spread out a mat in the same place I had the night before. I didn't think I was tired, but I underestimated the lull of the ocean combined with a day of sunshine and physical exertion. I must have drifted off to sleep because my eyes fluttered open to Jeremy lying next to me on a mat. Startled for the

second time in two days, I jerked back a few inches
hard wooden deck at my hip.

"Hey, sorry," he said, his face close to mine. "I
were playing possum and had to get nose-to-nose with you to see you were asleep."

"Oh, right. Sorry." I readjusted myself on the mat, tucking the blanket around me. "I guess I was tired."

"I'll let you sleep," he said, rolling over and presenting me with a broad expanse of back. "Good night."

I had to clench my fingers to keep from touching him. "Oh no, it's okay," I said a little louder than I intended. "I was looking forward to talking to you."

He rolled toward me again, a playful smile on his face. "Were you?"

I nodded. "I was. Am."

"Ah. But then we'll become friends and then we can't sleep together. You have that pesky rule and all."

I was still a little groggy from my catnap, but I was ready for him this time. "There are different kinds of friends," I said, willing him to hear the tone in my voice.

"Uh-huh. I see." He put his hand on my cheek and ran his thumb along my jawline. "I'd like to be your friend," he whispered just before he kissed me.

"I'd like you to be more than my friend," I murmured against his mouth. "You know, if you want to." And then it was several long, delicious moments before we broke apart to say anything at all because what started as a first kiss turned into a long, slow, sensual make-out session.

I came up for air, realizing my hands were tangled in his T-shirt and his hand was underneath the waistband of my leggings, cupping my ass. I could feel moisture collecting between my thighs in response to the erection pressing low against my belly.

He traced my lips with the tip of his tongue, his eyes opaque in the darkness. "So, a shipboard romance?"

"Uh...are you asking?"

"More hoping, I think," he chuckled. "I've been on a lot of boats and I've never found myself in this situation."

"I've never been on a boat in my life. What situation are we in?" I hooked my leg around his hip, bringing my crotch into full contact with the rigid length of his cock. "Because I really like this situation."

"Me, too."

I could forgive him for his lack of a witty comeback because he was making fast work of stripping off my leggings. A moment later, he cupped my bare pussy in the palm of his hand and I surged up against him like a fish on a line.

"It's a very nice situation to be in," he said, sliding down my body until the leg that had been hooked around his hip was now hooked around his shoulder and his tongue was slipping inside me.

I gasped and bit back a cry, intent on not calling attention to our amorous activities. It wouldn't do for the captain to make a sudden reappearance. Even if discretion was the better part of a valorous sailor, I wouldn't be able to keep the embarrassing predicament to myself and I'd never live it down once Laura and Gina found out. So I muffled my moans into my pillow as I rocked my hips against his mouth...his very talented mouth.

My orgasm came faster than I would've expected for a first-time partner. I didn't know if it was the thrill of sex with a stranger, the danger of possibly getting caught or his talented mouth—probably all three. As waves broke against the side of the boat, my orgasm washed over me with a gush of wetness that kept him lapping and stroking me for several long, slow minutes until I finally tugged at his T-shirt and pulled him up to eye level.

He smelled of me and, when I kissed him, he tasted of me. It was the most erotic moment of my life to that point. But it was about to get better.

He worked his hand down between us and pulled forth a plastic-wrapped condom. "I thought…maybe…"

I swallowed the rest of his words with another kiss before whispering, "Yes, now, god, I want you."

He was even quicker stripping off his own pants than he'd been with my leggings. A few seconds later I felt the head of his condom-covered cock pressing to my slick opening. He held my leg high on his hip as he angled into me and then, with a grunt from him and a pleased gasp from me, he was fully inside me.

"Oh god," he murmured, nipping my shoulder. "I'm not going to last long."

I laughed, flattered by his honesty. "It's okay. We have all week."

"That is not going to make me last longer."

I wrapped my arms around his neck and pulled him down for a kiss, undulating against him. "I want you," I whispered. "That's all that matters."

It wasn't the most ideal circumstances, but somehow we made it work, rocking slowly against each other on the thin sleeping mat. Still wearing T-shirts and mostly covered by my blanket, we might have appeared to simply be sleeping if anyone saw us at all. I pressed my mouth to the throbbing vein in his neck and tasted the salty tang of the ocean as his cock stroked my G-spot. Hiking my leg higher on his waist, I could feel the telltale gush that precipitated another orgasm.

"Oh, yes!" I gasped, rocking harder against him as his hands dug into my hips. "Right there."

He was quiet, his breathing harsh, and I could tell by the swell and jerk of his cock that he was right there with me. I clung to him, rolling my hips, nudging my clit against his pubic bone, awash in sensations that sent me over the edge and into oblivion as he moaned my name and went still inside me.

We stayed like that for several minutes, tangled up in each other, before he eased away from me to deal with the condom. He took me in his arms again, nestling my head against his shoulder.

"I'm not sure I can keep doing this and not at least be your friend," he said, tangling his fingers in my hair. "And I know we can't keep doing this if we're friends."

"Quite a conundrum." I tangled my fingers in his, my hair caught between us. "I may have to amend my rule about sleeping with friends."

"I think you will, yes. We have four more nights and then…"

"And then?" Sleep was tugging at me, but my pulse had quickened.

"Then I think maybe we should try this on land."

I liked the sound of that. A lot.

# THE LUXURY LANE

Sommer Marsden

"Happy anniversary, happy anniversary, happy anniversary… happy anniversary. My darling Rita." Timothy said every word up against the curve of my ear and by the time he was finished my neck was alive with electricity and I was laughing.

"Happy anniversary to you, too, Mr. Winters."

"I have a surprise." He hiked himself up onto the kitchen counter and swung his legs so his leather boots knocked against the lower cabinet door.

I cocked an eyebrow at him. He stopped.

We'd been married five years today. We'd gotten married young. Timothy twenty-one and me at twenty. People said we were rushing. We were too young. We'd never last.

People were wrong.

Our life wasn't high adventure. We weren't rich. In fact, we pinched every penny and cut every coupon. But my god we were happy and celebrating with him made my heart light.

"What is it?"

When he held his hand out to me, I took it. When he tugged me gently, I stepped forward between his spread legs and let him stroke my short, dark hair. Even though he'd mess it up and make me look like an asylum patient on the loose.

I laughed at the image.

"You're laughing and I haven't told you yet."

"I was laughing because you always play with my hair and I end up looking like I've been electrocuted."

Timothy grinned and ran his fingers full force through my close-cropped hair. Then he ruffled it even as I shrieked in our small yellow kitchen. "You mean like *this*?"

I batted his hand away. "Exactly like that." I tried my best to fix it and sighed, "You were saying?"

"I was saying I have a surprise for you. I think we should take a drive. And then, since we're poor, maybe the takeout section of Delmonico's. You can get your thing, I can get mine, we can come home and eat…naked."

I stood up straight—intrigued. "A drive?"

He grinned at me. The flash of his white canines never ceased to turn me on. They were very sharp and more than once we'd played werewolf and helpless heroine. I thought of those teeth on my skin, my nipple and lower and felt heat flood my cheeks.

"Yes, a drive. What are you thinking, dirty girl?"

"Nothing," I lied. "Tell me about this drive."

"We can take the Mustang."

"It's still undergoing a major overhaul," I said, tracing a small hole in his faded jeans with my fingertips.

"Yes, but she drives okay and where we're going there is virtually no traffic."

I blinked. "No traffic?"

We lived in a fairly busy city; the idea of no traffic anywhere was laughable.

"Yep. Once we get there it'll be us, the Mustang and a wide-open, empty road."

"Where are we going, Fantasyland?"

"The luxury lane," Timothy said. As he said it, he hooked a finger in the bodice of my orange sundress and peeked down at my breasts. He whistled softly.

"The luxury lane won't be open for months. Even years, depending," I laughed.

"Unless you work on it. Like your husband." He stuck a finger down into the bodice and swept it gently over my nipple making it stand up for him.

I made a noise that was half sigh, half purr and arched my body up to greet his touch. "So, what? You're taking me drag racing in the luxury lane? That infamous pay-to-drive lane that we all know will only be useable by the rich during crushing, mind-numbing rush-hour traffic?"

He nodded, pushed the fabric down and bent his head to lick my nipple. This time I did sigh.

"Yep. It's wide open. Mostly paved from where we'll be entering and we'll be the only ones there. It's Labor Day weekend. No working on the road. The state would have to pay through the nose for that one."

"And how are we going to get on?"

"I know a guy. He left just enough space between those orange cones for a '66 coupe to fit through."

He pinched my nipple and my mind went blank.

"Then Delmonico's and food and..."

"Naked eating," he said.

I nodded. "I'm in."

"Go put that dress on," Timothy whispered, pulling the fabric up and tucking my breast back in. I almost pouted. Almost. But thinking of flying down that pristine center lane that was intended to lessen traffic congestion for those who were willing to pay for access appeased me. “What dress?”

“The cream-colored one with the pretty gypsy print on it. The one that laces in the back—”

“You mean the one you like me to wear sans panties, that has a front that practically gapes so you can get your hand down in it?”

He grinned. “See, you know the one.”

Anticipation coursed through me and I went to put that dress on. That dress, with nothing underneath and lovely wedge sandals to go with it. I’d tuck a pair of panties in my purse for Delmonico’s. I didn’t bother with my short hair because it always looked like just-had-sex bed head no matter what I did and that was fine with me.

When we got in the Mustang and I buckled up, a small quiver worked through me.

“Excited?” Timothy asked, leaning over to kiss me. He put his hand in my lap, the warmth of it seeping through the thin fabric of my dress. It made the wanting worse.

“Very.”

“The road will be ours.”

“I know.”

“I can touch you at high speeds. Like I’ve always wanted to,” he said, winking.

I felt a flex deep in my belly and much, much lower. “I know,” I whispered. “Me too.”

And it was true. The last time we’d done anything close was when we were barreling down the highway toward Boulder, Colorado, to visit family three years before. In the cold, darkness of eleven p.m. I’d leaned over and unzipped his jeans and sucked his cock for a minute or two. Just long enough to turn him on, not long enough to make him crash. The mountains had crowded close over us that night, atavistic voyeurs to our exhibitionism. The mountains and a few big-rig drivers.

He took his time getting us to our destination. Driving lazily with one arm out the window as we headed toward the highway exit. I had to laugh. "Your practiced nonchalance is impressive."

"I'm wooing you with my cool-as-a-cucumber attitude," Timothy said, taking the exit with calculated ease.

"It's working. I think I'd fuck you."

"Oh wow!" He grinned, waggling his eyebrows at me. "I must be impressive."

When we came upon the ROAD WORK AHEAD signs, I worried. I worried that someone would be there. That a cop would be watching. That someone had moved the cones back to where they were supposed to be. But no. As we slowed and came upon the entrance, Timothy angled the coupe expertly and slipped between the orange cones. They appeared to be too close to allow a vehicle, but they weren't. Once we were in, I sighed, looking down the long, dark ribbon of highway uninhabited by anything other than some mobile signs flashing caution messages and freshly painted lines the color of spring marigolds.

He held up a finger, winked and reached behind my seat. A magnetic sign wobbled in his hand. It read STATE HIGHWAY CREW. He rolled down the window, slapped the magnet on the door and then popped the glove compartment. "Last touch."

A yellow cherry light for the roof. He hit the button so it spun and flashed, a lazy beacon that broadcasted the message *we belong here...it's okay that we're here...move along...nothing to see...*

I chuckled and put my hand on the fly of his jeans. Hard already. Gloriously hard. Hard and big and welcoming to my touch. I wanted to hike up my dress, climb in his lap and fuck him right there. Instead, I whispered, "Let's drive."

We drove.

He took the '66 up to eighty. Wind rushed through the windows and I laughed. "She shimmies at high speeds."

"She's an old girl," he said. "But still good. Solid steel. A bad ass."

His hand slipped into my lap, up under my dress. His fingers parted me as the car slowed some. He kept his eyes on the road and that added an impersonal, almost clinical air to the encounter that turned me on. He was intent and handsome and the years we'd been together felt as if they'd slipped by in a blink.

We had leveled out at about fifty-five, the road bare and smooth—virginal asphalt no one had driven on yet but to lay it and maintain it. I shivered a little.

"Cold?"

"No. Hot. Ready to come. Any second."

"Already?" he asked, glancing at me.

"Harder," I said loud enough for him to hear me over the engine.

He rubbed harder, knowing my body almost as well as I knew it. Pausing to skate his fingertips down along my outer lips, tracing around my clit without touching it. And then stroking me just as I needed. My dress up around my waist, head thrown back, cars beyond the Jersey walls streaking past in my peripheral vision. I arched my hips up to meet his touch. He slowed just a bit more, positioned himself so he could lean forward some and thrust his finger inside me. He thrust a few times before pulling free and spreading my wetness on my clitoris

I arched up again and when he punched the gas and the Mustang shot forward, my stomach dropped and my pussy clenched up tight as I came.

Timothy laughed. "There's my girl."

He stroked me softly for a few seconds and then primly smoothed my dress across my lap. We kept going. Driving with the southbound traffic—it was like flying.

The sun was a low red ball in the sky. I watched the horizon bleed colors that were dotted with only a few clouds. I unbuckled my seat belt and leaned over him. He'd worn button-fly jeans, my favorite kind. When I tugged the top button it pulled the rest of them open easily. Beneath the warm denim he was hard. And bare.

I laughed softly, pressing my face to his belly for a moment. "Were you preparing for me?"

"I was prepared for anything," he said, his voice fleeting from the force of the air rushing through the windows.

I pulled his cock out, shutting my eyes, feeling the speed we'd built up. Just to torture him, I ran the head of his cock along my cheek, over my lips, down my chin. My tongue stayed firmly in my mouth.

Our speed dropped a little and I smiled. He was always a cautious driver. What I was doing felt too good to go too fast.

I repeated the gesture, stroking my face and my closed lips with his cock before finally darting out my tongue to taste the tip of him. He was salty and warm.

Timothy's hips moved up just a hair. Had I not had my face in his lap I probably wouldn't have noticed. But it made me laugh. I parted my lips, dragged them along his shaft and swallowed him down as far as I could.

The wind whistled and Timothy groaned. Our car rocketed forward to nowhere as I realized I'd loved him for as long as I could remember.

When I sucked him hard he made a softer noise. When I ran my rigid tongue along that big vein on the back of his cock he sighed. When I sucked just the tip he groaned. I listed to his different sounds as they marched by. Every one made me smile because every one was caused by me giving him pleasure.

That was a power rush I never lost interest in.

When I tickled his balls with my fingertips and sucked a little harder he made a deeper, more animal noise and we slowed considerably and then drifted to a stop. I opened my eyes to darkness.

"Underpass," he explained in a rasp. The he tugged me up and toward him, unbuckling his seat belt as he did it.

With a thump and slide the seat went back and Timothy said, "Get in my lap, pretty girl. Hurry."

The urgency in his voice made me wetter than I already was. I climbed into his lap and stayed there on my knees, straddling him until he'd pushed the head of his cock into me. My thighs trembled with adrenaline and desire. When he pushed his fingers into my hair, hauled me in and kissed me, I sank down slowly. Taking him in an inch at a time until I was fully seated on his lap and we were both trying to catch our breath.

"Don't move," Timothy said. "Not yet." He tugged my hair lightly and kissed me again. He moved his hips back and forth almost imperceptibly. I felt my heartbeat in my pussy.

"Timothy—" I gasped. Then: "You're killing me."

"Okay, move, Mrs. Winters," he said.

I moved. Moving up as slowly as I could stand, sinking down with ease. All the while he did that thing with his hips that always made me mindless and frantic.

He released my hair to stroke my cheeks, my neck. His fingers danced over my collarbone even as he suddenly thrust up hard. I cried out and he bit my lip, stroked down my shoulders until he found my nipples, hard in the cooling air, and pinched.

"Fuck," I said for no reason but that I was overwhelmed with pleasure.

"We are."

The talking stopped and the fucking began in earnest. Timothy's hands migrating from my nipples to my hips where he held me tight and anchored me. My flouncy dress billowed around our laps as we moved and he broke the kiss, pressing his forehead against mine.

"Have I told you that I love you?"

"Every day for five years," I whispered, holding his shoulders.

"And every day for fifty more if I have my way." He drove up with a sudden ferocity.

I didn't have time to react beyond the crushing wave of bliss that crashed down on me. He kissed me as I came, swallowing my cries before giving in to his own release and growling as he came.

"Yes. For fifty more years. And many more than that," I said.

I put my forehead to his shoulder as he wrapped his arms around my waist to hold me close. Still locked together, still joined by love and so much more. I shut my eyes and listened to the rush of traffic and the rumble of the engine.

# JUST CAN'T EXPLAIN

Martha Davis

Women don't give in to their base urges. Some unspoken law in the battle of the sexes that, if I had any blood fueling my brain, I'd be able to recite verbatim. We are supposed to be coy with our physical needs. Men are hunters, have been since before they shed significant portions of their body hair and gave up walking on all fours. If they want us, they will come get us. If we like the effort they put forth, we will let them catch us.

I am the overachieving only daughter of Brazilian immigrants. A graduate of Harvard Law, the dictionary definition of the American dream with all the benefits and parental expectations that follow my station in life. Both mind and body are in a place where there's nowhere I can't go, nothing I can't accomplish, but repeatedly chanting that to myself doesn't seem to do a trace of good. It doesn't distract me, even the tiniest bit, from where I've centered all my focus, hard work, drive, and ambition lately.

"Hey, Malcolm," I said, answering my cell between the first

and second ring, unwilling to wait for the customary, more professional, third.

"Mmm, what are you wearing, sweetheart?" His voice purred in my ear, instantly soaking my panties.

I looked down at the white blouse buttoned to my throat, the black pencil skirt and matching shoes with comfortable office heels. Despite what I saw, I let sass improvise. "Wouldn't you like to know?"

"If you're locked up in your office with your legs spread and propped up on your desk, I definitely want to know. Every slow, vivid detail."

I considered pulling my skirt up over my hips and sliding my fingers into my panties, telling him how wet my pussy was, how the thought of his face slowly lowering between my thighs made my little clit so incredibly hard. That'd give him something to think about for the rest of the day, torture him like he insisted on doing to me. But at work, I didn't dare.

"Let me give you the address of a hotel downtown I want you to meet me at tonight, oh, say, nine-ish? What's that room number again?" He didn't pause long enough to see if I agreed. I heard a rustle of paper, then, "Oh yeah. Two thirty-one."

Malcolm was so confident I'd show up for his on-command booty call that he'd already reserved the room. And in an area of town with a well-known reputation—some cheap, dilapidated corner of Atlanta I would never willingly step foot in. Unbelievable!

"Elena honey," Malcolm said, filling the silence. "Do you remember how many times I made you call my name in the back of my truck the other night?"

"I didn't count," I lied.

"Well, I did. And tonight," his voice dropped deep and sexy, "I want to try to beat my previous score."

Fuck! I opened the bottom drawer of my desk, pulled out a spare pair of dry panties to change into when the call ended and slipped them into my purse. Oh, the things he did to me with his tongue while in the bed of that pickup parked behind the water reserve, with the sounds of weekend traffic on the highway below too close to ignore. Heat filled my face.

And I let him. Why do my hormones override common sense when it comes to that man? I'm a well-respected attorney at a prestigious Buckhead law firm and it would be in my best interest to try to remember that. If we had been caught? Hang up the phone. Don't give him time to think up something newer and dirtier.

"Elena, I adore you more than I can show you on the phone. Please come see me tonight."

He finally asked. Well, sort of.

"Okay." Damn! Where was my badass side when I need her?

All my concentration for months now had been focused on Malcolm Madrid. Well, if truth be told, on Malcolm Madrid's cock. I want to say it's the size that keeps me running back for more—he is nicely endowed—but I can't. He can last most of the night and rides like a jackhammer, but that's not what makes me answer the phone every time his number pops up on caller ID. Maybe his skill and creativity; who knew the mind and body were capable of such wicked things? But I have a vivid imagination myself and the means to afford an impressive vibrator collection that could probably do the same. There's just something about Malcolm, I can't explain it.

We first met at Underground Atlanta, the giant tourist trap downtown where the East/West and North/South lines of the subway system meet. I had just finished a quick lunch with a client and, afterward, used the unexpected free time to wander through its streets. Old-school streetlamps added ambiance to walls that still proudly bore bullet wounds from the war and the burn scars of General Sherman's march. Normal brick-and-mortar shops lined every inch of sidewalk and boxcart-style souvenir stands filled the pedestrian-only streets. The customers meandering everywhere were even more colorful and eclectic than the ones at night that came out when the bars aboveground opened.

I studied the college girl with purple hair who sold me a brownie big enough to rot my teeth on appearance alone and I felt him watching me from across the street. In a white linen, button-down shirt and jeans, the tanned, muscular blond looked out of place at the fortune-teller's stand drowning in vivid gypsy scarves and crystal balls.

He winked at me. I finished sucking the smudge of chocolate off my thumb, smiled and winked back.

He summoned me with his index finger and a come-hither gesture. I didn't comply, but I didn't look away, either. When he did it again, he mouthed the words, "You. Come here," as he took a seat in a metal folding chair behind a red-velvet covered table. Curiosity made me take those first steps toward him. He began shuffling a deck of Tarot cards and asked me to sit in a similar chair facing him.

"That's all right, sir. I'm not interested in a reading."

He looked up from the stack of cards. "Why not?"

"It's just not my thing. Thanks for the offer, though."

"Sit down," he commanded gently.

I quit being amused. I was raised to always be polite, but... "I'm not going to pay you for a Tarot reading. I don't even believe in this stuff."

"I invited you over. I wasn't planning to charge you."

I studied his chocolate eyes without comment. He blinked first.

"It's slow this afternoon. I'm bored and you're pretty." He slid the deck of cards to my side of the table. "Shuffle."

The way he watched me, with those chocolate-colored eyes, appealed in so many ways. Despite his physical surroundings and unusual choice in career, he intrigued me. I obeyed just to see what he would do or say next, but not without sarcasm. "Does your employer know you lure attractive women to your little cart here with the promise of free fortunes?"

"Benefits of being my own boss."

According to the cards, I was smart, hardworking and talented in my profession. Something legal? My future promised success in love, career, et cetera, et cetera.

"And you love brownies."

"The cards told you that?" I self-consciously wiped my lips with my thumb for any leftover smudges.

"This is not the first time I've seen you at that counter. I can feel your pleasure eating them all the way over here."

I continued watching his eyes without comment.

"Okay, you caught me," he said. "I admit to just guessing regarding the brownies, but the cards do say you will allow me to take you out to dinner one night this weekend." He handed me a professional business card with his name and contact information.

"You're really trying to pick me up?"

"Did it work?"

His cheeky smile grew so broad I could have counted every pearly white tooth.

"No."

"Then I'll try again. How do you suggest I charm you into going out with me?"

The hotel Malcolm told me to meet him at looked like something 1920s prohibition vomited up on a weekend bender and forgot. Fan of old architecture I was not, but complaints over the décor completely deserted my brain the moment I saw the blue van in the parking lot near the entrance. I was grateful the antique doorknob didn't fall off in my palm when I turned it and entered the front lobby, but that blue van meant only one thing. I gave my name to the receptionist at the front desk who seemed friendly enough and my presence appeared to satisfy her curiosity. Malcolm drove the blue van to meet me here.

"Any luggage, ma'am?"

"No." I shook my head. "I'm good."

"You're like me. I wouldn't plan on spending the whole night up there, either. Just going in that room after sunset makes you a braver soul than me." She pointed in the direction of the elevator.

I couldn't stop thinking about that van. My cheeks reddened at the recent memories of Malcolm baring my ass and spanking me, then fucking me so hard I felt his hands and cock several days after. Did the heat flooding my face come from the memory of that encounter or knowing how much I wanted more?

The strange looks and comment from the receptionist didn't faze me. In fact, I overlooked her curious expression until it was caught again in my peripheral vision when I stood at the elevator. As with the kinky sex with Malcolm, I'd grown too accustomed, too acquiescent. I knew what that blue van meant and the whispers between the receptionist and her coworkers returned my focus to non-naked matters.

The door wasn't locked. I let myself in and caught Malcolm setting up his camera facing a giant mirror hanging over the dresser. Tape recorders, both analog and digital, a heat sensor, and something he called an EMF meter, to measure the room's electromagnetic field whatever, were planted on every available surface except for the queen-sized bed in the center of the room. The bed had leather handcuffs at every corner like the grand finale of a leather version of *Debbie Does Everybody*.

Malcolm read Tarot cards and palms, he practiced candle magic—two white pillar candles were lit on the nightstand surrounded by lots of little tea-light-sized ones—and he was a professional ghost investigator. He used that blue van to haul equipment and his supernatural-seeking cohorts all over the Deep South in their need to contact Casper. That was, when he wasn't using it as available semipublic space to get naked with me. Had he summoned me here for an erotic rendezvous, or was this decrepit hotel nothing more than scenery for his latest ghost hunt?

Oh hell, I better not have shaved and "accidentally" forgotten my panties for a damn ghost hunt with his buddies. So help me!

"Hey, sweetheart." He gave my cheek a quick kiss. "You're early."

I looked around the room again. Better to say nothing at all than to say something that would bite me in the ass later.

"You're wearing my favorite red dress." He lifted my fists off my hips, urged them open, and pinned them behind my back in his hands. "That dress is too tempting to get any work done. I'm so hard for you right now."

He kissed me just like I liked, and pressed his erection into my lower belly, making my anger fade into nonexistence, but the pipes in the walls groaned and reminded me of where we were.

"Where's your crew?"

"It's just me and you." He looked slightly confused.

"So we're going to search for whoever's been here before us all by our lonesome?"

"Yes, ma'am. I trust you to protect me." He pulled away and

finished setting the camera on the tripod. "The ghost's name was Sarah Prescott. Local, turn-of-the-century, prominent banker's daughter socialite. She had interesting habits."

"So do you." I walked over to the bed and took note again of the hand and ankle cuffs at the head and foot. This was more along the lines of what I'd thought would happen tonight, but Malcolm was Malcolm.

"Sarah was a lesbian. Enjoyed dressing like a man and boinking hired girls in this very room. Lots and lots of hired girls. I'm surprised Daddy had any money left."

"The woman was horny." I caressed a cuff strap near the headboard. "I can relate." Cough, cough. Hint, hint.

His body movements responded like he didn't get it, but his smile revealed otherwise. "Because of segregation laws, the girls had to be sneaked in through employee doors. Like me, she preferred her women exotic, mostly of African descent."

"Like you?"

"Almost." He stood over me and studied my face and body, made no attempt to hide his interest. "I love exotic girls, too, but my preferences are more along the lines of cinnamon-kissed Amazon beauties with hair as dark as night and eyes that twinkle like stars."

Only Malcolm could find a way to be borderline poetic with no blood flow to his brain.

"And you, my beautiful Elena, are going to be the exotic bait I use to catch proof of her existence."

"Bait?"

"She has a reputation for voyeurism. Loves to watch couples have sex in this room. The rumors say if it's hot and kinky enough to keep her attention, she appears in this mirror I have the camera trained on. If displeased, she throws the lights and shakes the furniture up a bit."

"I'm not having sex in front of a camera." I shook my head to enforce my words. "No."

"The camera is focused on the mirror. We'll be heard, but we won't be seen. I know you, Elena." He sighed. "Believe it or not, I know when I've gone too far."

"But if she's a lesbian, wouldn't it be better if you got a lesbian couple?"

"She gets off on seeing beautiful women tied to her bed for her personal entertainment. The rest is irrelevant." He grinned. "And the candles are already lit in case she doesn't like hetero loving and shuts off the power again."

"Well, how many times has she been captured on film?"

"Never. But I've heard lots and lots of stories."

"Oh, please! I swear, sometimes I think you make this up so you can get laid."

I laughed. My smooth-talking, adventurous Ken doll looked athletic and strong, but not quite big enough to manhandle me. According to his crew, though, he could take one of me on each arm. That fact I forgot until Malcolm tossed me over his shoulder while I kicked and squealed protests, took three steps to the bed and gently tossed me into it on my back.

Before I could lift myself up to a sitting position, he pounced, pinned my upper body under the weight of his and held me down. We wrestled hard, laughing the whole time, until he took my wrists and pressed them firmly into the pillow with his hands. I couldn't move. I could barely breathe. My legs were splattered over the side of bed, spread wide, with my dress hiked up so high I felt the touch of the air-conditioning on my inner thighs. My pussy was so wet, I was sure it had completely soaked through to the mattress.

I tried to wiggle out from under him, but the smile he gave told me I'd only succeeded in making his cock harder. He maneuvered us in place, spread my arms and trapped each of my wrists in one of the handcuffs overhead.

"Do you know how really hot this is making me—you at my mercy?"

I tested the cuffs. They weren't going anywhere. I halfheartedly tried kicking free, but he made short work of cuffing my ankles, too. He spread me out across that rickety old bed like a human letter *X* in a barely there red dress, with erect nipples and a wet, swollen pussy.

"This bondage stuff is hot, but why don't we switch it up and put you on your back? Use your cock as a sundial for the coming dawn?"

"Ladies first." He pulled his shirt over his head and opened the fly of his jeans.

"Since when?"

"My lady, don't I always try to make you come first?"

Malcolm quickly covered my body with his, parted my thighs with his knees and kissed me senseless. He tugged down my bodice, exposing my breasts, and licked each nipple so long, made them so hard, I could have carved my initials in the headboard with them. The crevice between my breasts, he nuzzled with his nose as his fingers caressed my belly through the fabric of my dress.

He whispered, "Let me have you like this, sweetheart. I've always wanted to see you this way. Touch you like this." He pressed another kiss at my first rib. "If it's really too much I'll stop and let you go, but I really think you'll love it. You love being taken by surprise. It's the only way I can keep that fast-paced brain of yours entertained enough to come back for more."

I turned my head, but his curved index finger moved my chin into position where I could do nothing but stare into his eyes. I moaned with pleasure and melted like butter under the arousing weight of his body.

The lights from the camera caught in the mirror. "How did she kick the bucket?"

He bit his lip. He didn't want to tell me.

"How?" I demanded in my prosecution voice.

He pressed more kisses into my cheek and neck. "She fell in love. Allowed her lover to tie her to the headboard—tied instead of doing the tying—and once she was completely helpless, her lover betrayed her. Robbed and stabbed her. She, um, bled to death before she was found the next morning."

I pulled at the binding on my wrists. Sudden panic snatched my breath. I didn't want to hear any more, do any more. I pulled again, but it only reminded me how trapped I was, spread-eagle on a strange bed in a strange place with only the familiar weight of Malcolm's upper body pressing into me to provide comfort.

"Shh." He petted me, told me how beautiful I was, cooed sweet nothings until I quit pulling so hard on the restraints. "Just flow with it, baby. Feel how exciting it is. I've never hurt you and I promise, I never will."

My voice came out as part whisper, part growl. "I'm not going to make this easy for you, Malcolm."

He chuckled, "When have you ever been easy?" His hand slipped under my dress and pulled the skirt up higher. "You make me so horny I can't keep my fingers out of your panties." He put his index and middle fingers in his mouth, then moved them between my legs. "Oh, you're not wearing any. You're so wet. I love how wet you get for me."

He moved farther down, teasing me with his mouth on my lower belly and inner thighs, everywhere but where I wanted his mouth to go. Somehow I managed to maneuver the restraints to where I could trap his face between my upper thighs until my demands were clearly understood. If you tie me up, the least you can do is eat me.

He looked up at my eyes and smiled, then nuzzled the dark hair on my mound with his nose. He kissed me there and massaged open my pussy with gentle fingers. "You smell so good. You're so soft. Elena, I want you so bad I can't think..." His tongue licked a path his fingers had just finished drawing and when he found my clit, I choked down my last half-taken breath to keep from screaming so that the entire hotel could hear me. My hands clutched into fists and I pulled helplessly on the restraints wanting to braid my fingers in his silky hair and hold him in place until I came.

But I couldn't.

He did as he wished with my body and when he was satisfied tasting me, he sat up and took his cock in his hand, stroked it a few times and drove it into me hard and slow despite me being wet enough to allow fast, easy penetration. The fierce strokes of his hips between my legs and the gentle kisses and bites at my shoulders brought tears to my eyes. I wanted him to fill me up with his passion. "Please!"

"I need you, Elena." He sighed hard into my ear. "I need you to come for me." He pressed his lips on my earlobe. "I need you to come...with me. I'm so close, baby. Come with me."

Without losing rhythm, he reached over and took a candle from the nightstand at our heads and the moment my body started to tremble with orgasm, when I had reached the point where turning back was impossible, he lifted it high in the air and poured several drops of the wax on my sweat-smeared breasts causing the vibrations of my climax to intensify despite the slight sting. After a lovemaking session reading erotica to each other we once talked about playing with candle wax, but my opinion on the act hadn't been confirmed. I reached desperately for his shoulders, but the restraints only allowed for clasping my own palms. His orgasm followed right behind mine. He groaned hard and collapsed over me.

For a moment, he looked over at the bits of wax and then at my face. "I didn't go too far, did I?" he asked softly.

"No."

"When I bought the special low-heat-burning candles at the store today, I thought pushing your boundaries and causing intense emotion might incite our ghost." He kissed a wax-smeared pink spot right just above my breast. "But if truth be told, I love inciting you, watching you get all fiery."

He kissed me again, so gently his lips were barely there. "I love you, Elena," he whispered and buried his face in the crook of my neck. "I love you so much." We lay in bed like that, with him still inside me, for what felt like an eternity. I thought about him, impossible not to, tied up beneath him with his body so much a part of mine. He had consumed my whole world in just a few short months. Where was this going? What would happen next?

We spent the entire night in that bed making love, never once getting up other than to turn the equipment off. He never said the words again and behaved as if they were a mere whispered thought. But I knew he meant them. As flaky as he was, he never said anything he didn't mean or did anything he didn't want to. Malcolm Madrid was pure and good and wholesome. Every time we made love after that first time, I put my hands on him, wrapping my arms and legs around him, just like I'd longed to do the entire time he had me tied up.

The camera somehow wound up in my car instead of Malcolm's van. I found it in the backseat when I stepped out of the office for a drive-through lunch and brought it back inside with me along with my purse and salad.

The possible contents of that camera wouldn't leave me alone. I don't believe in ghosts, but Malcolm believed, and I wanted to share his world. I hoped for him, with all my heart. Let there be an image on his fancy camera screen that fulfills all his supernatural ponderings and let me be able to give it to him. I locked the doors and flipped it open.

"Do you know how really hot this is making me—you at my mercy?" All those moans and groans. Who knew we were so noisy? The mattress squeaking made my hands suddenly lose interest in the salad on my desk. They found their way into my panties, where I teased open my pussy and worked magic on my clit. Masturbating in the office while watching homemade porn. And you know what? I just happened to think it wouldn't be the last time, either. If I came really hard, I'd have so much fun calling Malcolm and telling him all about it.

Then she appeared, a barely there reflection in the mirror, a platinum blonde with unforgiving eyes. Obviously, she wasn't as pleased with her room being used as a make-out point as Malcolm's legends liked to believe.

"I love you," Malcolm whispered in the background and it warmed me all over again.

Sarah Prescott's face softened. A single tear glimmered almost invisibly on her cheek and she vanished. I tried playing it again. Nothing. But it had been there. I saw it! Again. Nothing but hints of the globes of Malcolm's bare, fuzzy ass bouncing. The only sounds were mine and his.

I told Malcolm when I returned his camera. He watched. Saw nothing.

"You have to believe me! Sarah Prescott was in that mirror!"

"I believe you, sweetheart." He petted me. Obviously he didn't. My argument wouldn't hold up in ghost encounters court without evidence. "It's okay, love. We'll do it again any time you want. I know this place in Marietta that sells the most intriguing bondage equipment. Let me take you there."

"But I don't think she was there to see the bondage games. She responded when..." She responded the moment I was willing to go past the boundaries where I felt most secure and powerful, where I wasn't so confident in my step. And I was rewarded with love. Malcolm's love.

Sarah had opened her heart and surrendered to an act of love that wasn't love after all. I did the same and—he's eclectic, he's goofy, will never be typical lawyer bait—but he's every bit the Prince Charming I always dreamed of. It wasn't his off-the-charts career and hobbies, his never-ending sexual imagination or even his magic cock. I loved Malcolm Madrid. And he loved me. Sarah Prescott had found what she was looking for in that mirror, made her peace and signed out permanently.

"Malcolm, I love you." His eyes and smile grew. I pulled him down by his shirt and kissed him with everything I had. "I love you. Let's go shopping at that store you suggested. This time, we try one of my ideas. You know I've always wanted to..."

# THE COUCH

Malin James

Daphne drifted along the edge of the party, murmuring the odd hello. She hadn't wanted to come, but her husband, Tom, the diplomat, had gently brought her round. Then he'd been called out of town, again, which is why she was going alone.

Annoyance compounded the ache in her head. This was the fourth time in three weeks he'd been suddenly called away. It was the nature of his work, she knew, but she missed him, especially at an event like this.

The dress she wore clung like a spill of dark chocolate as she moved from room to room with a glass of champagne dangling from her hand. She wasn't in the mood—not for champagne, and not for parties. As soon as she'd greeted her hosts, she would make her excuses and leave. Nick and Kate were lovely. She was sure they'd understand.

A waiter with a tray of martinis stopped and offered her one. Gesturing at her untouched drink, Daphne shook her head. The last thing she wanted was a cocktail. What she wanted was a cup of tea and an orgasm before curling up in bed. Daphne thought of the vibrator in her bedside drawer and frowned. She missed Tom. She really did.

Salon. Music room. Hall. Daphne finally found her hosts—another diplomatic couple—in the library, after wandering through what felt like a game of *Clue*. Mrs. White in the ballroom with the razor-sharp wit... Daphne's mouth quirked.

The library was surprisingly large for a residential home, even one so near the embassy. Brass reading lamps shed dim pools of light, while, above the fireplace, a nude gazed down at the massive leather couch. Daphne paused. That couch really was something—more of a bed really—and big enough to be just a touch indecent. Even to Daphne's distracted eye there was something debauched about it, as if it had been made with no other purpose than to cradle naked flesh. Briefly, she wondered how often Nick and Kate fucked on that couch. Quite often, she suspected.

Daphne scanned the room. Nick and Kate were tucked off to the side, just beyond the light of a miniature Tiffany lamp. Nick's hand, she noticed, was caressing Kate's thigh beneath her pale beaded dress. Daphne raised a brow, suppressing a coil of envy. But before a thought could properly form, a man walked into the room.

He was tall—very tall—which Daphne noticed immediately, being quite tall herself. He was handsome in a sort of unexpected way, narrow and compelling, like a large, sleek cat, and his dinner jacket and tie were crisp, as if they'd just been pressed. But it was his eyes that fully engaged her. There was a sweetness to them, visible from across the room, that made her forget the vibrator in her drawer.

*Tom,* she thought. Her stomach flipped. He should have been in Singapore.

Daphne's body began to hum, but she controlled the impulse to wave. He hadn't called, which meant that he wanted to surprise her. She didn't want to spoil it for him.

Drifting back against a bookcase, Daphne watched his blue eyes scan the room, calmly, pleasantly searching. A furrow formed between his brows, and her heart swelled a little bit. Then his gaze came to rest on her and he relaxed into a smile. He had two drinks, one in each hand. *Such beautiful hands,* she thought as he crossed the room, weaving lightly between a thin scattering of guests.

"Hello, lovely. What are you drinking?" Soft, familiar lilt...

"Champagne," she said, as her brows arched playfully, "but I wouldn't mind a martini."

He gave her a wide-open grin.

"I happen to have one right here."

He gave it to her with mock deference and she couldn't help but laugh. It was a low, surprising sound from a habitually serious mouth.

"Like magic," she said, taking a sip.

"Well, I couldn't leave you standing there all alone with a glass of unwanted champagne."

Daphne cocked her head. She was thrilled but confused. He'd never cut a trip short. Happy as she was, she didn't know what to think...and then there was the fact that he hadn't kissed her yet. Leaning in, as if he'd read her thoughts, he tested the waters before brushing her mouth with his. It was tense and a bit unhappy—more conversation than kiss.

"I'm sorry, love. I missed you. I always do."

They sipped their drinks, eying each other over the rims, as he angled his body ever so slightly toward hers. Hyperaware, hypersensitive, she angled her body toward his.

"When did you get back?" she asked.

"Less than an hour ago. I came straight from the airport."

Then Tom kissed her again, slowly this time, tongue darting lightly against hers. It was like a first kiss—their first kiss—five years before. Daphne sighed, as her headache began to fade.

"How long will you be home?" she asked, and immediately wished she could take it back. There was an apology in his eyes. She didn't want to know.

"I'm sorry, love, not long. I have to fly out in the morning."

The headache came thundering back. She had him for the night, and it was more than she'd expected. But, still, she wanted more.

"I see," she said, hating how cold she sounded. "You're lucky, you caught me then. I was thinking of going home."

He considered her.

"Can I convince you to stay a bit longer?"

Daphne smiled. She couldn't help it. He was so earnest and serious. They were such a pair.

"Perhaps. Just a bit."

He placed a hand lightly on her back as their bodies swayed, subtly negotiating the terms of their attraction. She knew he was giving her space, which was the last thing, really, she wanted. They already had too much space. Acting on impulse, Daphne set her drink aside and rose up on her toes. Then, very gently, she nipped his ear.

"I missed you, love," she said.

Tom went still. Daphne smiled, knowing she'd hit the mark. She eyed the deep, leather couch, which was inexplicably empty. In fact, the entire room had emptied, though the door was still ajar.

"Would you like to sit," she asked.

"Yes," he said. "I would."

Daphne allowed Tom to guide her across the room. She loved

the way his hand rested lightly on her waist. Savoring the warmth that pooled between her legs, she leaned into him a bit.

The couch, when they reached it, was even bigger than it looked. She sank into the buttery leather and crossed her legs, feeling like Goldilocks in Papa Bear's chair. In fact, if she were prone to giggling she would have. Instead, she watched Tom sit down beside her—just close enough to catch a hint of his aftershave. The scent went straight to her head. She felt light-headed, and drunk, though she'd barely touched either the martini or her champagne.

His eyes met hers, and she smiled, allowing the edge of a promise to curve her lips, as she leaned in. God, he smelled good.

"Are you as hard as I am wet?"

Tom narrowed his eyes. She wasn't usually so blunt, but they only had one night. She wanted Tom, and she wanted him now.

"Say again?"

Daphne shifted, settling her long legs several inches from his. His eyes flickered down over the bare length, and, for the first time that evening, she saw naked heat flare in the genial warmth of his eyes. Civilized Tom. Nothing civilized there. Pushing her advantage, she leaned in bit farther and purred right against his ear.

"Are you as *hard* as I am wet?"

"I thought that's what you'd said...."

Daphne held her breath as Tom kissed her neck, sparking pleasure through her skin and right into her bones. Her spine flexed, drawing her close.

"I've wanted to fuck you since I left Singapore."

Daphne's breath caught. Tom had never said he wanted to *fuck* her before—make love, of course, but never fuck. Daphne turned her face, and nuzzled his lips.

"Kiss me, then."

The kiss was like him—warm and lovely—with a solid edge beneath. He was holding himself back. Normally, she loved that, loved that he had so much to offer that he could hold some in reserve, but right then, she wanted what was simmering beneath. She wanted more of that edge.

"Do you want to leave?" he murmured against her mouth. He tasted of gin and her perfume.

"No, I don't," she said. She had come to the party alone. Thanks to this development, she saw no reason to leave. Not yet.

"I want you to make me come," she said, "right here on this couch."

Daphne felt his lips curve against her skin.

"Let me close the door...."

"No," she said. "Leave it alone."

Slowly, Tom settled back.

"Are you sure?"

Daphne nodded, loving the mixture of concern and lust in his eyes.

"I'm sure. Now, make me come."

Tom laid her down. The couch hid them from a casual glance, but anyone could have seen them if he walked into the room. A fresh gush of heat pooled between her legs as Tom shifted and kissed her again, but driven by her awareness of the open door, Daphne pushed past his sweetness and nipped his bottom lip. He stiffened, surprised. Then he smiled and nipped her back.

Daphne let her hands slip down from his waist to his hips, which were pressed lightly into hers. She could feel him through layers of silk and wool. He was hard and getting harder despite his easy, playful mouth. She arched against him. He felt so good, fit so well into the cleft between her thighs, that her body began to move, a soft undulation at first, and then a demanding grind. His breath hitched. With a grimace, he lifted his hips away.

"Careful, sweet. Or you'll ruin the game."

She smiled, enjoying his admission as he parted her legs and half reclined between them. Then his hands began to move. Nerve endings fluttered between her legs as her nipples peaked, achy and hard. She tilted her head back and sighed. He touched her as if he had a map of her in his mind…he had always known how to touch her.

Tom stroked her thigh and coaxed her legs open wider, as the silk of her dress pooled just above her waist. Instinctively, Daphne's abdomen contracted and her hips tilted in demand. He smiled and kissed her cheek.

"Easy, love. We'll get there."

The words dropped into the hollow of her ear, electrifying her skin from collarbone to scalp, and sending a shot of aching heat straight through to her cunt. She bit her lip and gripped his lapel, but he'd already moved on, slipping down the straps of her dress to expose her lovely, teardrop breasts.

Daphne shifted, restless beneath his deliberate hand. She was already going mad, and he hadn't gotten anywhere near her sex. Words formed in her mouth, but she could only gasp when he dipped his head and took her entire breast in his mouth. He suckled hard, flicked her nipple with his tongue as she, so reserved, so habitually quiet, moaned. *I sound like a whore,* she thought. But she couldn't help herself.

Her fingers threaded through his hair, sealing his mouth to her breast. Nip, kiss, and then a brutal suck as he pinched the rosy nipple of her other breast. Daphne's eyes glazed, and her body twisted. She was nothing but nerve endings now, crackling and sharp, while her cunt was a syrupy pool. He murmured something, but all she heard was the lilt of his accent. She shook her head, responding without knowing what to do, as his hand slid down her body and toyed with her lace-covered sex. She whimpered and gripped his shirt, crumpling his lovely starched collar, as she kissed his neck and suckled his spicy skin. She wanted to gobble him up.

Clever fingers stroked the lace before pushing her panties aside. When he touched her swollen folds, she nearly jumped out of her skin.

"Are you sure you want this?" he whispered.

His voice had lost its smooth, rounded edge; his accent was more pronounced. His was stroking her more firmly now, dipping his fingertips into her slit and slicking her juices over her delicate, swollen skin.

"I want this," she said, tilting her hips and inviting his fingers in.

Her leg quivered and her muscles tensed as he slid one, two, then three fingers in. There'd been an ache in her since he'd left—there always was—and his fingers were soothing it. She hated missing him....

Daphne reached between them and found his cock through his pants, suddenly desperate to feel him. He moaned and grabbed her wrist. Very deliberately, he pressed her hand above her head and held it there against the soft leather of the couch. Then he kissed her, hard, bruising her lips, leaving nothing in reserve, while his other hand kept stroking the walls of her channel, harder and deeper, until she felt like she couldn't breathe.

She was soaked, his hand was soaked, as he slipped a fourth finger in. She moaned, arching her back as the blood rushed to her head. Playing her body like a musician, he let go of her wrist and stroked her clit with the thumb of his other hand.

Her hips bucked, meeting him hungrily as his fingers fucked her harder, deeper, caressing her in places that she couldn't even name. He was breathing heavily now. Sweat sheened his brow, but his eyes never left hers, though her vision had hazed and she could barely see his face.

The pressure built in her, fast and hard, throbbing in her blood. She needed to come. She couldn't bear it. She writhed and clawed his wrist.

"Please," she whispered.

"Yes."

The word hung full between them, as he pressed down on her abdomen with the heel of his hand. Then his fingers found her G-spot, and Daphne's body snapped as pleasure jolted through her system.

The orgasm poured through her, ebbing and flowing, filling her lungs and limbs. Unable to bear it, Daphne cried out, as if the sound were being extracted, manually, from her chest. Then Tom's mouth covered hers and he kissed her, swallowing her pleasure whole.

He let her ride the climax for long as she could, slowing his movements in time with hers until she calmed and went still. Daphne sighed, eyes closed, a sweet smile on her lips. When she opened them, she found him watching her, eyes warm and sweet and inviting. She reached up and stroked his face.

"Are you all right, love?" he asked.

She smiled. "I really missed you, Tom."

"I missed you, too, Daph."

Tom got up carefully, while Daphne draped the hem of her dress over her naked skin. Then he held out his hand and, placing hers in his, she allowed him to lift her up.

"Shall we?" he asked.

"Yes," she said. "Let's go home. You can tell me about your next trip."

# AGAIN

Axa Lee

I've got my hands up on her hips, laying lazy kisses across her chest. My eyes meet Rhys's across the dance floor. He's sitting at the table, watching us. His eyes are scorching shadows in the dim bar light, made dimmer by too many half-priced Long Islands. She smells like Pink perfume and sweat, making me want to lick her all over. Her hands are all over my ass, teasing up the edges of my tight skirt, finding the tops of my thigh-highs. Her mouth quirks and she gives me an appreciative smolder when she realizes I'm wearing a garter belt but no panties.

"She hasn't been able to keep her eyes off you all night," Rhys said when Gwen went to get us all more drinks at the bar. I shoved his shoulder, which had no effect on him whatsoever. Teaches me to date an athletic guy.

"Shut up," I said.

"I can see why." He had to speak beside my ear in order to be heard over the band.

The band played old Stones songs. They weren't bad either, giving the old tinny chords a more rockabilly sound. "Some Girls" was followed by "Champagne and Reefer."

"You look fucking hot."

His fingers skimmed the low neckline of my clingy, lacy top. He groaned his appreciation of the ample view of cleavage.

His eyes smoldered when they met mine. He leaned in to bite my ear at the same time his hand drifted over my ass. He loved it when I didn't wear panties in public. Shivers ran along my body and I melted against him as he breathed into my ear.

We've been together too long; he knows too well what I like.

And tonight, I liked Gwen.

"She's hot," I said.

"Go dance for her," Rhys said.

At the bar, Gwen half turned. She caught me looking at her, half-kissed the air in our direction before turning back to pay the bartender.

I turned back to Rhys, my eyes seeking his. "You don't mind?"

He cocked his head, smirked. "Babe." And that was all he had to say.

Sudden shyness hit me.

"I can't," I said.

He set his hand on my ass, squeezing the sculpted muscle there. "Dance for me then," he said, and then growled in my ear. "Move that sexy ass for me, so I can think of how sexy you are later when I'm fucking you while you're fucking her."

The pang slammed all the way from my ear to the floor of my pussy. I loved how he talked dirty, told me explicitly what he wanted to do to me and how, and how much. It was such a fucking turn-on to not have to wonder what he was thinking.

Another song started, a faster one this time. I kissed Rhys, hard, open-mouthed. He flicked my tongue like he was going down on my mouth. I smacked him, a playful smile on my lips, and bounced off his lap.

"You have my phone in case my dad calls?"

"Yes, honey, go."

I wound my way to the center of the crowd, writhing my body in time to the music. The bass beat through me, and I gave myself up to it, letting my body absorb the music and respond, not thinking, just feeling and grinding. Before long I felt someone behind me. I felt the smooth touch of slinky clothing, not the raging hard-on from some roadie. Her hips welded against the hard curve of my ass and we rolled together, sinking and rising, rotating and gyrating in slow, deliberate synchronicity.

Gwen was exactly the type that did it for me—tallish, fit, stacked, femme but still looked like she could take care of herself, well-dressed and manicured, *coiffed* I think is the term, the kind who oozes confidence, that sort of casual "I know I'm sexy," who wears it without acting conceited. As well as being a drop-dead gorgeous redhead. I'm a sucker for a redhead. Like Rhys.

The song ended and flowed into the next. I turned. My arms went around her waist, and Gwen's fingers tucked a bit of hair behind my ear that had gotten loose from my messy style. We smiled.

She was a friend of a friend, someone we had met two or three times before, who'd just broken up with her ex. We'd been out bowling with mutual friends, Joe and Ashlyn, and Gwen made a half-drunk comment about only fucking girls or couples from here on out. It had started as a joke on a Thursday night, and here it was Saturday and my hands were all over her body.

The music had changed to a sultry rendition of "She Was Hot."

Gwen snapped one of the straps on my garter belt.

I scoffed, half in disbelief at her and half in lust.

Gwen bent to shout beside my ear. "Your man—he likes to watch?"

I shook my head, smiling lasciviously. "He likes it *all.* He likes what makes me happy."

Gwen's eyes traveled down and up the length of my swaying body. She ran her hand along my side, down to the swell of my hip. I shivered.

"And this makes you happy?"

"Very."

She smiled.

And then we did no more talking, letting the music carry us, while my man, my generous, wonderful man, watched from the table with a smirk on his lips.

I had my hands up on her hips, laying lazy kisses across her chest.

My eyes met Rhys's across the dance floor.

She has a great smile: pouty, kissable lips, and her eyes lighting up. I love that. She's willowy but somehow voluptuous at the same time. She has that smile and full-bodied laugh that makes me think about laying her down and taking her breasts in my mouth. I want to explore her wetness and her smooth skin, to nibble her mouth and bury my tongue in her pussy. I'm hoping these urges aren't written all over my face. It's one thing for Rhys to notice, because he notices everything, especially when it comes to me.

She's got me so hot and bothered, all I can think about is taking her home. The night has a pleasant haze from the half-priced Long Islands and I can't believe my lust isn't dripping down my leg. It's painful to stay upright in these heels, which press my thighs and pussy lips together. I'm so swollen it's agonizing.

I've never heard "Paint It Black" sung this way, with the barely restrained vocals of a female singer. She has the kind of voice that crawls through you, husky and huge all at once.

"You should get your man out here," Gwen says, nodding toward Rhys. Like a good boy, Rhys has remained on the sidelines all night, letting us girls get acquainted. But this is a date. Gwen knows it. And knows that she'd be dating both of us. The chemistry has to work in all three directions.

We beckon him to us and all dance together. Rhys doesn't switch, first me, then Gwen, then back, and neither do we; somehow we all seem to move together, complementing one another. It's this, the undulations of our bodies, that seals it. I couldn't point to one thing or one moment, just at one point I know: this is going down.

Gwen must feel it too, because she leans in and says next to my ear, "I'd love to eat your pussy."

I shiver and cream, letting my body flow against hers, saying with body language what I seem unable to speak out loud.

The song ends and I keep ahold of her hand.

She and Rhys work out the logistics on our way out of the club. Rhys gives Gwen a companionable hug and ducks around the side of the car to start it.

"I just have to ask you," she says, leaning in a little, "would it be all right if I kissed you? I've been wanting to kiss you all night."

Her lips are soft. I've kissed girls before, so I expect it, but each time I'm surprised by exactly how soft another woman can be. I shudder as she touches me, pussy aching painfully, as though we've established a direct line from our lips to my cunt in our sexy dancing all night. She drags her lips over mine, enough to make me whimper, then opens her mouth and devours mine, her hands on my ass, dragging me against her. I kiss her back with just as much hunger, and when she breaks the kiss, I'm disoriented for a few moments.

"Damn," I whisper.

She groans, our pelvises still pressed together.

"You have such a tight little ass," she says, giving it a squeeze. "I love it." She winks at me. "See you soon."

I fall into the car, head spinning, and give Rhys a big, dopey smile.

"She's hot," I say.

"Come here," he says and pulls me to him, crushing my mouth to his. "I wanna be inside you so bad right now, baby."

Luckily we don't live far from the bar because almost as soon as we get through the door Rhys has me pressed against the wall.

Of course it's then that my dad coughs and sits up, waking from where he fell asleep watching RFDTV on the couch.

"Eh?" he says. "You two back, huh? Have fun?"

I detach myself from Rhys and try to play down the flush up my neck and chest.

"What time did the baby go down?" I ask, though our eighteen-month-old can only be considered a baby by the thinnest margin.

"Eight-fifteen. On the button. Just like you said. Busy little bastard." My father sounds gruff, but his eyes glow when he talks about my son. "I'll pick him up tomorrow for some man stuff, huh?"

I love my dad, but am desperate to have him gone. I'm shaking, so much so that I'm afraid he'll notice; the hitch in my voice, the cold trembling of my hand. I need Rhys, desperately need him inside of me, and Gwen will be here momentarily. But I force my voice to calm. For a moment, I need to be a grown-up, not a hormone-fueled basket case.

"Sure, Dad." I smile at him. "Man stuff" usually consists of taking him for ice cream and playing with his toy tractors.

He leaves and Rhys has me pressed against door, hands on my ass, breathing hot down my neck. I shudder, breath hitching.

"I want to be inside you," he breathes beside my ear. "I want to fuck your pussy while you eat hers."

The buzzer sounds and it's Gwen. Rhys groans and rips himself away from me.

We should give her the apartment tour, I know that. As good hosts we should show her around and point out the view of the city and the size of the kitchen, exclaim on the lowness of the rent since they're trying to get these loft apartments in Old Town rented quickly in a city betterment project. She should exclaim over the adorable baby toys that litter the apartment like little landmines. We should offer her a nightcap, make awkward small talk, watch "The Daily Show," until my hand snakes up her thigh and we start kissing again.

We *should* do this.

We should, and she should, but...

But instead when she walks in the door and I take her coat, when Rhys goes to make drinks in the kitchen, I can't help reaching up to cup her cheek and kiss her. That's how, when Rhys returns with the drinks, I'm pressed into the leather couch and Gwen's hips are slowly grinding into mine, our mouths slanting hot against each other. The drinks are set aside, redundant, and not too long after I find myself in our bedroom, bending down to kiss her, with my legs braced across hers where she sits on the bed.

Gwen's lips are supple beneath mine. I drag my fingertips down the backs of her bare arms and she shudders. She presses her mouth harder against mine, nipping at my lower lip. I feel her smile against my mouth. I'm absorbed by her soft moans, her startled gasps. They get me wetter than I can remember being with anyone, besides Rhys.

Clothes are shed, rustling and falling to the floor, forgotten.

It took me a long time to not think we were deviants or bad parents, for wanting to find another woman to share our bed, for leaving our child with a sitter while we went out. But, as Rhys pointed out, our son and his grandpapa loved each other so the boy was well cared for and if we were happy and he didn't get hurt, that didn't make us bad parents. Just different ones. And as far as the two of us sharing a girl, I knew we could handle it. We're just that kind of couple.

Rhys's hands cup my ass, then squeeze, and he presses against me. I feel his hard cock against my ass and combined with the raw passion in Gwen's kiss, they have me shaking. Rhys kisses along the back of my neck and places a lingering bite on the meat of my shoulder. Heat rushes between my thighs and I'm so wet and swollen that it hurts.

I press Gwen back onto the bed and we scoot around to a suitable position. She kisses me with a barely restrained enthusiasm, all but devouring my mouth, and I kiss her back just as voraciously, cupping one of her spectacular breasts in my hand. The softness of her body contrasted to the harder planes of Rhys thrills me.

Rhys lies down behind me and begins to finger me. I'm so swollen and wet that I cry out in wordless ecstasy, biting back being too loud.

"I love you enough to share you with another woman," Rhys had said. We were lying on the couch after bowling on Thursday, my underwear gone and his pants still open. It was as far as we made it before collapsing. My dad had babysat that night, too. Under Rhys's touch my skin rose in goose pimples as he drug his fingers up and down my bare arm.

I snorted. "Most men would."

"No, seriously," he said. "I don't want to fuck her. I want to fuck you. I love you. I want this for you. I want you to be pleasured and I don't even care if I come."

He knows this is a hang-up with me. I'm convinced a guy has to come every time to be happy.

He's not.

"Feeling you come so hard that your legs don't work, getting you off that hard every time, that satisfies me," he's told me.

"What kind of mutant guy are you?" I asked, but I'm secretly pleased. I'm even more pleased those times when he can't control himself and comes inside of twenty minutes, when after one of my big orgasms he loses his own control, having just felt me come unbelievably hard. I love that I get him that hot. So this is as much for me as it is for us. "I still feel like we're bad parents though."

"Our son is being taken care of by someone he loves. We know this girl, and she's not a psycho or anything. As long as we don't wake him up he won't even know mom and dad had a friend over for a playdate."

"As long as we're sure we won't forget about her," I said when I was able to stop laughing. We're a little into each other, and have joked that a third might feel left out when we really get going, gazing adoringly into each other's eyes and fucking like we love each other.

It's not a worry I should have had. Not with Gwen at least. She's not the type to let herself be ignored.

Her kiss shoots through my lips, sending electrical thrills through my core. If she's the lightning, my body is the rod and I feel her charge all the way down my spine.

Gwen's body is a candy land to explore. Her ripe pink nipples; her waxed pussy. She tastes like grapes and light champagne. I tongue her folds, tasting her wetness, nuzzling my face against her thigh. She emits soft exclamations of pleasure as I stroke and taste and tease. Her first orgasm is a light one, where she gasps and moans, fucking my mouth until her legs shake. I'm tonguing her clit and Rhys reaches around me to stroke her to orgasm, one long finger sunk into her pussy. I lick my man's finger where it meets her cunt, soaked in her come, and smile up at him. He grabs my ass, hard, and thrusts into me with the middle finger of his other hand. It's so abrupt and I'm so turned on that I start to come almost immediately. I climax around his hand and collapse onto the bed beside Gwen. She and I pant and laugh breathlessly, both of us sheened with sweat.

Rhys's hands trail over my body.

"You can touch her," I say, then look to Gwen. "If that's all right with you."

"I'm game," she smiles. "Your guy's hot."

I straddle Gwen's hips while Rhys leans down to kiss her. I feel a pang, a good one, as my man kisses this other woman, as his hand clenches on my thigh. I know the feel of his mouth, the feel of his kiss, but to watch it takes it to some other place for me. Maybe there's a little voyeur in me, but all I know is that it gets me sopping wet to watch my man kissing the woman I've just been kissing, while his fingers travel up my thigh, to hear him groan against her mouth when he encounters my wetness.

He turns his face up and I bend, kissing him, tasting her on his lips. She does a half sit-up, dragging her teeth along my neck, biting my ear. I groan.

"Now fuck her," Gwen orders.

Rhys needs no other prompting.

I groan as he pushes inside me. The fullness of his cock makes me clench and quiver.

Something magic happens whenever Rhys enters me. Lock

and key seems an über-cliché, but it's true. Other keys have been close, and even done an all right job, but something with Rhys gets me to come almost as soon as he enters me. And no matter how debauched we get, even when he's whispering filthy things in my ear and fucking me doggie-style with a finger on my clit, I feel loved and safe. Thus the orgasms are spectacularly overwhelming. And this one, one of many, is no exception.

Gwen, meanwhile, is stroking me, kissing me, reaching to touch my clit, where Rhys and I are connected, feeling our flesh sink together over and over. It's so hot that I scream into her mouth as I come, though I'm still conscious of the little green lights on the baby monitor. But I give myself over to the rocketing, vibrating orgasm, holding on to her and Rhys for dear life, stars dancing in white pinpricks of light behind my eyes. Rhys stifles a shout, thrusts into me one last time, biting my shoulder as he twitches inside me.

None of us can catch our breath for a while. We lie, arms and legs entwined, Rhys behind me, Gwen and I breast to breast. Rhys's fingers trail up and down Gwen's back, then interlace with mine when our hands meet against the plane of her back. Rhys brushes his lips along the nap of my neck.

"Can I confess something?" I say to Gwen. "That was our first threesome."

"Oh," she says, in the same tone anyone uses when she realizes she's taken someone's virginity. I feel her draw away for the briefest of moments, then she snuggles against us, even tighter than before.

"I just have one question then," Gwen says as she resettles herself. "When do we get to do this again?"

# FERTILE

Jade A. Waters

"The bitch is in heat."

Sheila rolled over, letting the mountain of blankets fall away from her face. When Jerry stared down at her, his lips twisted up in the same grin he often gave her this time of the month—the small window marked in pink highlighter on the calendar hanging opposite their bed.

"Ouch, Jerry," she grumbled.

"What? I was talking about the dog."

"Sure you were." Sheila blew her hair out of her face and slipped back beneath the covers. It was easier to ignore her husband and focus on the internal workings of her body, as if she could hear her ovaries screaming their quiet, ticking warning: *It's time, Sheila! Don't you want another one?*

But every time the window rolled around, Jerry was too busy poking fun at her.

"Hey." He curled himself around her and slid his hand beneath the sheets. He honed in on the subtle canyon between her thighs, and Sheila tried not to jump when he shoved his palm right up against her. "You're so sexy when you're raring to go like this," he said. Jerry crept his fingers under her panties for a momentary graze of her tender lips, carrying the stroke down and back up, warming her in an instant. Sheila released a heavy sigh. For all his teasing, Jerry had possessed radar for her sweet spots since their first night in the back of his pickup truck ten years ago.

"Do you want to, Jerry? Don't tease me..."

"Do what?" He latched his lips on her ear, the slow flickering of his tongue almost erasing his earlier taunt.

"You know what." She waited, then whispered, "Baby."

Jerry grunted, his tongue off her ear faster than the two syllables had taken to come out, and when he crawled out of bed, Sheila nearly screamed.

He cast her a glare and adjusted his pants. "You push too hard."

Sheila tugged her knees into her chest, her pussy wet and her lower abdomen contracting in that telltale way she was lucky enough to recognize. *Ovulating.* This time, she couldn't decide if she was more frustrated with knowing that they were going to miss the window due to Jerry's stubbornness, or that he'd left her sopping like a dishcloth in under thirty seconds before climbing out of bed.

She didn't speculate on it long. Daniela barged through the door, all wails and giggles and "Daddy, please, breakfast?"

Jerry caught their four-year-old and planted a kiss on her cheek. "Sure thing, darling." He gave her a few tickles, sending Daniela into hysterical laughter that brought a smile to Sheila's face. She was the perfect daughter, conceived on the first try during a picnic under the stars, the exact way they'd wanted it to happen.

*So why aren't we letting it be as perfect this time?*

Jerry set their daughter on the floor with a gentle pat on her bottom. "Off you go. I'm right behind you!" His adorable daddy skills stirred Sheila further, and she calculated how many hours until the highlighted window would once again pass them by.

Daniela charged out the door and Jerry winked at Sheila. He made a quick tap of his fingers against his lips. "Soon. Very soon. I promise," he said.

"Right." She threw the covers back over her head as the door snapped shut.

It wasn't that they didn't love each other anymore, or even that they didn't have any spice in the last four years. Though, heaven help her, strapping herself into some of those frisky little costumes from the lingerie store had zapped her hormonal longings before she ever crept out of the bathroom to give Jerry a show. Her body wasn't what it used to be before Daniela stretched her stomach to oblivion, but she'd bucked up and tried it anyway, ignoring her subconscious criticism all the way through. And even with their daughter bursting randomly into the room—a habit they really needed to work on since Sheila kept trying to fuck the daylights out of her husband in order to make a second munchkin to burst into their room—no romantic issue was barring them from making this baby. Plus, they had always said more children. From their first date they had said two or three, but Jerry seemed inclined to make fun of her whenever the time was near.

Sure, he touched her. Good *lord* could he touch her, bending her this way and that as he fucked her like only two people who had known each other for over a decade could. Jerry had been sending her into ecstatic heights since the first time he stared into her eyes and thrust inside her.

But now, it never happened in the right window, convincing Sheila that she and her husband had distinctly different plans for the arrival of their second child.

"Are you going to get up, or what?"

Sheila leveled a gaze at Jerry. He stood at the door, his work files in hand, and another innocent grin on his face.

"I don't feel like it."

He laughed. "God, you're fussy."

Sheila rolled her eyes.

Jerry set his files on the dresser and walked back to the bed. "Daniela's got her cereal and a big glass of milk in front of the television."

"I thought we agreed no more TV in the morning?"

"Yes, we did, but it seemed important this time." He leaned into the mattress, his weight making the bed slope slightly in his direction.

"Why on earth…?"

He shrugged. "I told work I'd be late because of a doctor's appointment today."

Sheila rubbed her face and peered at the calendar. Nothing was marked on it, save for the daunting spread of highlighter and stars around today's date. "What are you talking about?"

Jerry tugged the covers away to stare over her half-naked body.

"You're my appointment," he said, "but only if you stop being so damn pushy." Sheila didn't quite understand what her husband was saying until he'd grabbed her hips and pulled her sideways. Her legs fell over the edge of the bed and he stepped directly between them.

"I am not!" His earlier comment nagged at her, but the way he wrapped his hands around her thighs and slid his thumbs along the crease at her hips drove her temperature up.

Way up.

"You are." Jerry dropped to his knees and laid one hand over her panties. The heat of his palm radiated through to her sex, and Sheila huffed. Her body, as usual, was determined to control her, ignoring the frustrated woman in her mind.

"But you've been making such a big stink about *not* messing around. You've kind of been an ass." She considered moving away, but Jerry's gaze swept down her legs to her feet, then back up her exposed belly and breasts. There he hesitated.

"I know I have, but so have you." He chewed his lip. "I'm not a baby machine, Sheila. Sometimes, I swear, you make me feel like that's all I'm good for." He cocked his head, his eyebrows wrinkling together to enhance the creases of his forehead. He'd had them back when they were young, too, but years of work, of life, of chasing after Daniela, had deepened them.

"Jerry—"

"Shh," he said. "Let me finish."

She tried not to squirm as he grazed his fingers over her. Under the cotton of her underwear, she throbbed for him to touch her. She was baby-crazed, yes, but his touch was magnetic and every inch of her craved him more. Jerry still hadn't finished his thought, so she muttered, "Are we seriously going to have a conversation with your hand on me?"

"Yes." He dragged his fingertips down, tracing the shape of her lips, and Sheila trembled as her moisture seeped through the fabric to encourage him. He lifted both hands to the elastic edges of her panties, shoving his fingers inside and resting them over the coarse patch of hair she needed to trim.

Sheila gasped.

"I can take them away right now if you want," he muttered. He tore his gaze from her soaked panties and looked into her face. "And I'm sorry for teasing you, but you can't pressure me like that. You can't treat me like I'm your sperm donor, babe. It's the most cliché bullshit in the world."

"I don't..." She really didn't, but the pained look on his face made her cringe. His hands, meanwhile, were making it impossible to have this conversation. Her hormones had become a raging inferno that made nothing but his touch important at this moment.

"You do." Jerry crept his fingers farther, straight toward her aching entrance. Tiny tendrils of heat burned down her thighs as he snuck one finger inside and barely tickled her with the end of it.

"Jerry," she whispered. She wanted his whole finger, his whole hand, and then, the hard bulge she knew he'd formed in his pants. He'd always been ready to go at a moment's notice, making his extended delay to give in so much more frustrating.

Instead of answering, Jerry pressed his mouth over her, on top of his splayed fingers. His breath came through the fabric like a gust of hot wind, sending goose bumps over her chest. He paused, his mouth so dangerously close she was ready to tear off her own panties if he didn't soon.

Jerry pulled back. "I know I've been bugging you for months, partly because you get so flustered, but also because you've badgered me."

"Because—"

He cupped his mouth over her and she moaned.

"I know why. And I did want what you want. I do want it, but dammit, Sheila, treat me like your husband." He grabbed the top of her panties and shook his head. "Like you want me because I'm a man, not a machine." He inched the elastic waistband down over her hips and Sheila pressed her hands to her face. Embarrassment burned in her cheeks and down through to her core, and when he just kept staring at her, she trembled. "Do you understand what I'm saying?"

She wanted to believe she couldn't understand much of anything with her sex exposed to the cold air of the room, but watching Jerry—this beautiful man, the father to their child, the one who had worked so hard so she could stay at home with Daniela like she'd always wanted—she could see why he had teased, and why he had pulled away for so long.

"I'm sorry," she said.

"I am, too." Jerry nodded, then let her panties drop to the floor.

Sheila sucked in a breath and lay still. The hormones pummeling her nerves demanded she pay attention, but she wasn't about to ignore Jerry's frustration. Not with his eyebrows knitted together and his lip caught between his teeth as he pondered his next move.

"Jerry?"

He didn't say anything, then reached up to grasp her hips. He laid his mouth over her, this time covering her completely.

"Oh god."

Jerry flicked his tongue over her clit. "Do you want more?"

Sheila forced her head up. "Do you have to ask?"

He slicked his finger from her swollen nub to the base of her slit. "Tell me, then." When he drew his finger over her, his expression softened. "I love the way you look right now, but I need to know you want it."

"Yes, yes, I want it," Sheila said. "I do."

"Because the way I see it, we're in heat, but if you really want me—"

"Jesus, Jerry, yes!" Sheila shimmied down on the bed, attempting to thrust herself over his finger.

He groaned. "Do you?"

She closed her eyes. Every inch of her skin begged for him. She clenched inside, trying to draw his finger in farther. "Yes, please. I want you, all of you..."

"So, I've got this wife all bothered, and we have some time to spare. Or at least, as long as it takes for our daughter to get bored with the 'toon channel."

Sheila laughed, but Jerry shoved his finger so deep the sound shifted into a moan.

"Ten minutes?" she murmured.

"At best." Jerry caressed the bundle of nerves he always found inside her so easily, every time. He tickled her there, scratching with the tip of his finger before easing a second one in. "I don't even need that," he said. He lapped at her folds and stroked his fingers in a deft symphony, riling her up so fast she gritted her teeth to keep from screaming out lest their daughter hear. A cloud of hunger filled Sheila's mind, and when Jerry took his hand away to open his zipper, she panted.

"Now, honey, fuck me." She pushed her hips up, aching for him to return. "I want to feel you," she said.

The smile on Jerry's face was wider than she'd seen in a long time, and he lay over her with his pants low on his hips. When he pressed against her opening, he whispered, "What do you say we make a baby?"

Sheila groaned, her hands on his ass in seconds as she tried to draw him closer. Her crazed morning stupor washed over her—a combination of worry over their daughter walking in, confusion for his change of heart and a longing for him to plunge forward and take it all out of her mind. But the thoughts melted away as he plowed inside, coating himself in her wetness.

"Fuck, Sheila!" Jerry shuddered on top of her, and her eager cries brought his lips crashing into hers.

He thrust forward, burying himself inside her while they

moaned between kisses. Every inch of his cock rubbed against her, filling her in that familiar way, but this time with a purpose that drove them in a shared, hungry fervor. *For a baby.*

"Jerry, yes!" His shaft banged high inside, striking harder than she expected but delicious all the same, and her thoughts came as a jumble of *baby* and *horny* and *I love you* and *fuck*. She pictured him inside her, their lovemaking more than love but actually committing the ultimate act of union, and the thought made her walls begin to shake. Jerry's breaths grew frantic, matching hers, and he sank deeper as she bit his shoulder to tame her calls.

"Yes, honey, yes," she whispered. Her building excitement made all the other thoughts impossible to hang on to, especially once Jerry slipped his hand between them. He kneaded her as her panting amplified—and then his pattern grew steady, the same one they knew would send her over the edge after years of practice, in, out, hold, in, out, hold, in. Her face began to numb. Sheila cried, "Jerry yes, I'm going to—"

She didn't need to say it, her breath taking over her words and Jerry driving, drowning himself in her as she came. They rode her trembling together, Jerry grunting and dragging his hands over her breasts, his body quivering as he came right after her. Sheila moaned when his warmth filled her. Maybe, just maybe, it would grant both of their wishes.

Jerry gasped and dropped his head to her chest.

"Holy fuck."

She chuckled, savoring the slowing contractions her body made around his length. When her husband raised his eyes to hers, they were glazed, half slits that struggled to remain open.

"You are so hot when you want it," he said.

She brought her hands to his neck, rubbing them under the collar of his work shirt. He'd need to change before he left, his clothes wrinkled and smelling of her, of sex, of the mission they'd finally tackled.

"Well, I guess you finally caught the bitch in heat."

They both laughed until Daniela called from downstairs—something about milk on the carpet—but Sheila didn't mind.

Jerry dragged himself away then, weaving in a lusty stupor to find a new shirt in the closet. "I'll handle it, if you promise one thing."

She rolled onto her side, her hand tracing the curve of her belly as she imagined the little one they'd create. If not now, then later. *Soon enough*. "Yes?"

"How about we put Daniela to bed early tonight so you can show me how much you want it again?"

Sheila smiled. "Deal."

# ALL YOUR TOMORROWS

Skylar Kade

Fifteen months of tomorrows. When I was in high school, those days spanned the eternity between the start of senior year and college. After college graduation, it marked the countdown to my wedding.

A tear slid down my cheek and I snatched it into my palm. I had promised Tom I would not cry. We had said good-bye. We had come to terms with the whole sordid affair. But every time I turned the corner of Willow Avenue and spotted our house at the end—every time I relived The Call from his doctor that rang right in the middle of this intersection fifteen months ago—it struck me anew.

Tom's beloved 1969 Chevy Camaro shuddered with me as I shifted gears. It was his wedding gift from me, a rusty piece of junk he lovingly restored over ten years. A beautiful memory, replacing stark images of him wasted away in a hospital bed. Another bitter tear slipped against the corner of my mouth.

Something grinded—in my head? Under the hood? The car

shivered again halfway down the street, a stone's throw from home, then sputtered to a stop.

A puff of smoke wafted from the engine.

Dead.

*He's dead, Taryn.* The doctor's words screamed in the silence of the still car.

My head sank forward onto the steering wheel. I didn't care if it was five o'clock on a workday and my neighbors would bear witness to every movement as they returned from their offices. I didn't care about anything except not fully losing my shit in public. I estimated the distance from here to my front porch, calculated the boulder in my throat and determined I wouldn't make it. I was going to have my nervous breakdown right here. Fifteen months' worth, because that's how long I was able to keep my promise to Tom.

*Don't mourn me, Taryn-love. I'm ready. Promise you'll keep on. Live enough for both of us.*

I had gone back to work, though my home office rang with the emptiness of the house. I had redecorated, donating everything of Tom's except the car, needing all of the painful reminders out of the house. I had adopted a chocolate Lab puppy who made me get out of the house every morning at 6:00 a.m., then a Manx cat who claimed my lap as his possession, then a cockatiel whose only words were *hey pretty mama* and *sexy thing*. I didn't ask who'd owned him before me, because in the North Hollywood area sometimes you just didn't want to know. I had ignored the little strip of lawn in front of our townhouse because the last time I'd had to mow grass, I was earning allowance from my daddy.

Thank god for my neighbor, Jacob Gill, or the HOA surely would have booted me out by now.

*Speak of the devil.* Dodgers cap on his head, replica jersey unbuttoned around a navy-blue T-shirt, he exited the townhouse three doors north of ours. The one right next to my car, as bad luck would have it. The other neighbors would have let me wallow. I didn't think Jacob rolled that way—he'd retained just enough Southern gentleman after his fifteen years in California to be a nuisance to the natives, as he liked to say over dinner, back when Tom and I hosted our regular poker nights.

At that moment, I would have killed to be a pretty crier. The movie-star kind, where the eyes got all misty and that beautiful lone tear tracked down a razor-sharp cheekbone. But not me. I was more the lost-teddy-bear toddler, complete with burning, swollen red eyes and the occasional snot bubble.

I grappled for a handful of napkins in the glove box, detritus from my last round of In-N-Out, and dabbed at my face. I wouldn't win a beauty contest, but at least my nose wasn't melting all over my face.

Armed with the soft smile and kind eyes he'd had for me since the funeral, Jacob knocked on my passenger-side door. I rolled down the window. "Car trouble?" He gestured to the tendril of smoke that curled from the hood.

"I think she's—" I choked on the word, swallowed, then forged ahead. "She's dead, Jim." I couldn't help it. We'd been huge "Star Trek" fans. The inside joke just happened.

Jacob's bark of laughter swept aside the awkward moment of *I'm not pitying you, I swear* that built every time I mentioned mortality. He reached for the car handle. "Beam me up, Scotty?"

A genuine smile spread my damp cheeks, rare as a red shirt who survived planetary exploration. I reached across the seat and popped the door open.

I'd forgotten how big Jacob was. Easily six feet, with shoulders broad enough to fill out the jersey in a way that had interest flickering in the pit of my stomach. "What time is the game?"

Since he didn't dress like that every day, I assumed the Dodgers were playing at home.

He didn't look away from me. "Doesn't matter." So matter of fact, and as weighty as his attention. "How about we push this sucker to your driveway?"

I grabbed the distraction, ignoring the guilt for making him late for the game. I needed to not be at home, alone, right now. "Only if you let me thank you with dinner." I gestured to the backseat. "Lasagna's about the only thing I don't burn, and the craving's been building for weeks." Only then did I remember his plans. I rushed to backpedal. "I'll leave a couple slices for you, pick them up after the game."

He laughed and patted my hand where it rested on the shifter. "I bet it tastes better straight from the oven."

I struggled to ignore the wash of sensation where our skin touched. When was the last time I'd felt…anything? Loneliness swamped me. While the pets fulfilled me, offered something to look forward to every day, it wasn't the same.

"Think I'll stay for dinner." Again, Jacob brushed aside the awkward silence. Grateful, I offered a tremulous smile while I tried coming to terms with the hermitage I'd built around myself. He would be the first person I entertained in the house since Tom's wake. Did I even remember how to play hostess?

I didn't know—did a polite hostess ogle the muscled biceps of her guest like she'd never seen a man in person?

Ten distracting, sweaty minutes later, I was no closer to being reassured, but I was calmer. We'd gotten the car in the driveway. I'd snuck a couple of jarring looks at Jacob's butt in the tight jeans he wore. Turns out I was still a woman, and no sane, straight woman would be able to resist that view.

Jacob popped the hood then grimaced. "Cracked radiator, looks like."

I winced. We'd replaced a cracked radiator on my little Honda once, and it had hurt the checkbook. I was sure some dedicated car enthusiast would be happy to take this otherwise cherry Camaro off my hands....

And that's when it hit me. I had well and truly lost Tom. Aside from a single box of keepsakes in the attic, the car was all I'd kept. The rest hurt too much, living in a space marked so clearly as *ours*. Now it was mine, all mine.

Too mine.

Was it fair for me to feel betrayed all over again? Like dealing with his death once wasn't enough—this piece of him had to abandon me too.

Fuck fair. The loss ripped at the stitches of my torn heart.

I thunked down onto the bottom step of the porch and, for the second time that day, bawled. I was scooped up against a broad chest. Two strong arms wrapped around me, held me close.

"Shh," Jacob whispered. "Let it out."

He carried me to the porch swing. It crowded the whole veranda, overwhelmed the front of the townhouse, but I didn't care. I sat on it and watched the sunset with a glass of wine, drank my coffee there after a long walk with Frankie, and now, in the arms of a man who wasn't my husband, I mourned. Jacob had been a good friend and better neighbor since we moved in. He'd always made me laugh and touched me with his thoughtfulness. There had even been innocent flirting, as I assumed he did with all women.

Maybe I had been wrong. I couldn't see him pushing cars and forgoing baseball games and dealing with crying jags for just any Mary Sue.

As he stroked my back and let me cry onto his jersey, I stopped thinking of this man as *Not Tom*. He became Jacob: warm male body and comfort and contact and...need.

Wrung out from my sob fest, I crushed my cheek harder against his chest. The dark, woodsy scent that rose from his skin embedded in my lungs.

As if it rushed in to fill the vacuum left by purging all those built-up tears, longing subsumed my body. I tilted my head up, taking in the strong, square jaw covered in day-old stubble. What would his skin taste like? Would it satisfy the ache in my belly, the kind that was only soothed by indulging in a forbidden craving?

Our eyes met. My need was reflected in the hazel depths. Only they weren't gentle now—his eyes burned with all-consuming heat. It hit me in the solar plexus and I gasped.

"Taryn, I don't—" His jaw clenched and his arms banded tighter across my torso, misinterpreting my shock.

I wasn't going anywhere—he didn't need to hold me in place. I pressed a finger to his lips and let him see my intent. With one hand on his corded forearm and the other resting against his cheek, I let my body ask. My soul chaffed from isolation.

With an exhaled sigh, Jacob pressed his lips to my forehead. I fought back tears brought on by the tenderness. "Inside." I started to rise, but he clamped down, then lifted me once more. "You stay right there, darlin'."

Damned if I would fight him on it. Being held was too good to give up yet.

Somehow he managed to take the keys from my pocket—my stomach flip-flopped when his fingers brushed across my thigh—and unlock the front door without dropping me.

Frankie greeted us with happy woofs from his room on the bottom floor and I caught sight of Minx sitting in front of his door. Taunting or keeping company, I could never tell. For now, they would both need to wait.

Jacob knew the house well enough, between helping me move

furniture around after the big purge and pet sitting during my occasional business trip. He dropped the keys in the dish by the door and strode through the foyer to the stairs.

Our breath mingled as he climbed; his from exertion, mine, anticipation. I hoped I could attribute some of his heavy breaths to that as well, but that remained to be seen. Was this a pity fuck? Jacob was a thoughtful, sweet man, but it wasn't like he'd be hurting for company.

Just past forty, Jacob had aged well. Silver touched his temples and small lines winged his hazel eyes. Too many smiles, too much time outdoors hiking the foothills north of Los Angeles. It certainly didn't hurt his physique, as my body—so different from his, soft where he was muscled, curved where he planed into sharp angles—could attest from its up close and personal attention.

I refused to believe I was so pathetic and guilt inducing that he was doing me a favor, throwing me a bone. Literally. Besides, he'd done a swell job of comforting from afar. If mowing the lawn hadn't made me crush on him just a little bit, the gift basket he'd left on my porch three months ago cemented it.

I'd tried not to make a big deal of the anniversary of Tom's death. In fact, I had done such a good job ignoring the date that it snuck up on me until I woke that morning and remembered. Dead inside from grief, compounded by the guilt of almost forgetting, I'd slogged through my morning motions.

When I got back from my walk, a small gift basket sat on the porch. There was a note: *My grandmother used to say life was like chocolate—a little bitter, a lot sweet. And when you read this, I hope it's not in Forrest Gump's voice :) —Jacob*

The basket included a box from Godiva, cocoa, and chocolate liqueur. Cures for every mood I vacillated between that day. I clung to the memory of Jacob's beyond thoughtful gift. A man, no matter how much a gentleman, didn't go out of his way like that for just anyone.

He settled us onto the soft brown couch I'd purchased after Frankie and Minx destroyed the leather set that had sat in the living room since we'd purchased the house. I looked up from my position on his lap. His gaze snared me and I forgot how to breathe.

It might have been ages since I'd last seriously flirted with a man, but there was no mistaking Jacob's intent. Heat flowed through my veins like melted chocolate.

"I am going to get the groceries and let Frankie out. You are going to sit here and look pretty. Okay?"

I nodded. My hair was a wreck, my eyes still burned from the tears and I was in my work uniform of yoga pants and a soft knit top. I looked a mess, but his words left no room for doubt. In his eyes, I looked pretty.

Thank god he'd left before I swooned. How had I let myself go so long without simple affection? Flirtation? Sexual attraction?

The now-silent house reminded me. Loving and losing once had nearly broken me. Going through it again? I'd chosen to remove the possibility from my future equation. The fear crept back, cobwebs from an old abandoned house. But one night wouldn't change anything.

I wouldn't let it. But I could seize it, store away all those touches and kisses and intimacies to tide me over.

He returned and I watched with an avid, greedy gaze as he moved seamlessly through the second floor. Cold and frozen groceries were stashed on random fridge shelves but I could not care less about the disorganization. Task completed, he closed the distance between us.

Fingers knotted together, I stared at his lips. His eyes told too much. The lips kept things firmly in the one-night stand camp. I started to speak, then stopped, having no clue what to say. Again, I let him take the lead, needing to be guided back into this routine, not that it had ever been one of mine. A handful of sexual partners, all except one in long-term relationships, had seen to that.

The thrill of unexplored territory helped balance my uncertainty. I reached out a hand for something solid—for Jacob. He met me halfway, then tugged me to my feet.

He cupped my cheeks in his warm calloused palms. "You are so beautiful, Taryn. So strong."

I gasped, wanting to protest. He shushed me with the gentle brush of his lips across mine, searing deep as a live wire. The shock reached parts of my body, my brain, that had long lain dormant. It could have been a mere kiss between friends, it was so brief.

It was so much more.

My clothes, moments ago so comfortable, now trapped me. I needed skin contact, like I could absorb through osmosis all the vitality he exuded and make it my own. "I need—"

"I know. Me too, darlin'. God, me too, for so long." His fingers slipped under the hem of my shirt and I cried out. Arching closer to him, I rubbed up against the thick length of his erection. It shorted out my brain until my only thought was of feeling him inside me. That burn and stretch, the melding of two bodies—I couldn't breathe past my desire.

We left a trail of clothing from the living room to the guest bedroom on the same floor, stripping in a frenzy of hands and kisses. Formerly my craft room, I'd converted it to a bedroom when sleeping upstairs was too stark a reminder of loss. The top floor was all mine now—walls torn down to create one open workspace with sunlight pouring in from windows on three sides. Making love up there in the middle of the day, lounging in puddles of sun during postcoital cuddling, would be sublime.

I shut down that thought as his teeth closed on my earlobe. There would be no lovemaking, no future with Jacob. Sex, yes, but I couldn't contemplate the risk of anything else, as much as I craved human companionship. That was a want. Tonight was about addressing a need for sex, hard and blissful and cleansing.

"Stay with me here. That's my girl."

At his words, I refocused, not wanting to miss a moment. He stroked a hand across the curve of my ass. His nails barely scraped across the skin, giving me a bare edge of intensity.

"Keep me here." I challenged him to give me something more than the sweet sex I'd had in my previous life. I'd schismed along with the Camaro's radiator, a jagged line between the woman I'd been and the woman I wanted to be if only for tonight, unafraid.

Jacob backed me to the wall, trapped me there with his body. "That's the sweet fire I love."

My heart jolted at his casual use of the word. I shied away from the multitude of meanings and implications, refusing to play that game of reading between the lines. Instead, I buried my fingers in his thick chestnut hair. It was as soft as I'd imagined, which was shocking in itself, recalling that I had wondered what his hair felt like. I'd been aware of him long before my conscious mind realized it.

That galvanized me into action. Too many months of asceticism, trapped by guilt that I wasn't grieving the "right way."

"Jacob—"

His kiss made me forget how to speak. Firm lips stole my breath and his tongue danced along the seam of my mouth until I granted him entrance. His groan vibrated through my chest and my nipples hardened.

I thought I'd be ashamed, being naked with a man again. His lust left no room for anything but offering the same in return. Our kiss spiraled on until the world spun around us, with Jacob as the one solid point in my reality.

His hand unwound from my waist and skimmed down, over the arch of my hip then dipping across the soft skin of my thigh.

I parted my legs, giving permission for him to take more. And take, he did.

Expert fingers slid across the wetness that had pooled at my entrance. I cried out as sparks lit through my body. Lazy, slow, his fingers explored my dips and hollows, finding the edge of my clit that made my breath catch and eyes sink closed.

Pleasure rose higher and I would have been adrift in this new-old place if not for the solid strength of his body against mine. Even the hot line of his erection nestled against my hip steadied me. He wanted—I could feel that—but it didn't rush his movements. Such a gift.

One finger slid inside me, tight, so tight, but the pain was good. Unfamiliar. Distinct. He sank deeper within me, then retreated. His thumb danced circles around my clit, keeping me buoyed on pleasure. With each pass, my body accepted him more easily until he added a second finger and all that bliss crashed down. I moaned his name and dug nails into his scalp, clinging to his hair as he drew out my orgasm.

Wrung out, I would have sunk to the floor if not for his body pinning me against the wall. Jacob planted kisses along my collarbone, neck, cheeks...anything he could reach from his towering height.

I hadn't eschewed all pleasure in the past months, far from it. But no orgasm from my own hand had rocked me like that. Greedy, I wondered how many more I could get before he went home tonight.

Step one—make it to the bed. I pushed against his shoulder, then looped my hand in his so I could draw him to the queen mattress in the corner. "I think a bed would be advantageous from here on out."

And I was so right.

Jacob wasted no time spreading me out on the soft navy sheets, working my body into a frenzy once more with fingers and lips and tongue. And when I thought he'd drawn all the possible pleasure from my body, only then did he settle over me.

I braced for that first penetration, more nervous than I had been losing my virginity in college. He held still and waited for the truth to crash through my plasterboard walls.

And crash it did. Jacob's every reverent touch was a sledgehammer to the barriers I'd erected.

He wouldn't be satisfied with this night, not if he crossed this final line. And, god help me, neither would I. Every kiss had been a stark reminder of what I'd given up. Every brush of his fingers, a taunt. Every orgasm, a tease of what I could have if only I were strong enough.

Jacob brushed a strand of hair off my forehead, then pressed a kiss there. Too much, too honest, too true. I squeezed my eyes closed and arched my hips, hoping we could take this back to safe territory.

"Look at me, Taryn."

I couldn't deny him, not after he'd so thoroughly claimed my body. "Just tonight, please, I can't..."

His soft laugh rumbled across my flesh. "Yes, you can."

I shook my head in denial. He saw everything I couldn't say—so why did he insist I vocalize it all? "Scared."

"Of course." He wrapped me up in his strength and let me shiver while his weight pressed me into the mattress, safe and warm and protected. "I'm not asking for all of your tomorrows—just one. Can you give me that? I think lasagna was promised somewhere." I stole reassurance from his little smile, the one that lit up his eyes and made his laugh lines stand out against the tan landscape of his face.

"You're in—in this situation, and you're thinking about food?" I bit my lip, loving how he'd pulled me back into safe territory. Tomorrow wasn't scary. I'd tacked together my recent existence on *one more day*.

"Darlin', I might be a gentleman, but I'm still a man." He nuzzled into my neck as I laughed. "So what do you say? Dinner tomorrow?"

"Only if you promise to make tonight worth all the effort of making you dinner from scratch." My smile was reflected in his.

"Deal." He swooped in for another kiss.

Like my assent had been the starting gun he'd waited for, Jacob's hands raced along my skin. He hooked one arm under my knee to cant my hips up. With the other, he braced above me. I nodded to his unspoken question and he slid into me, melding us together.

"Waited so long for this. God, Taryn—" he stuttered and the words ground to a halt, but I could feel his intent.

I gathered my bravery, bolstered by his honesty, his closeness. "Me too. Worth it, huh?"

He groaned in assent. "Yes, but this is just the beginning."

I didn't dare protest, though the thought crossed my mind. But Jacob's soft kiss was my undoing. How could I argue with his potent blend of stubborn tenderness and intense pleasure?

The pace shifted, galloped along with my heartbeat. His even thrusts hit something good, so good inside me. I gasped, grappling for him. My teeth dug into his shoulder and then it was all too much. I cried out as he rolled his hips to press deeper, harder, until he was coming too.

When he left the bed to clean up, I pulled the sheet around my ears. Cold and sated and edgy, I waited for him to dress and go.

"Not so soon. It's almost midnight, and I think you promised me tomorrow. I'll just stick right here and wait for it." He tugged the sheet from my grip and scooted beneath until he was spooned up against me.

Into the wee hours of the night, he held me as I cried out the last of my guilt and sadness. Finally, after fifteen months, I was ready to fulfill my promise to continue living.

And Jacob would be by my side tomorrow.

# THE CROP

Claire de Winter

She comes home burnt to a crisp—fourteen-hour days, clients on the phone demanding attention, boss in her office daily asking for reports she has no time to write. Doesn't he see, she wonders, the stacks of paper, her assistant running in and out, the email pinging, the phone lighting up? She'd been living for Friday since Tuesday, and now here it is. Peace.

She takes off her tall boots and thin socks at the foot of the stairs and somehow feels freer as she trudges up barefoot, bypassing the kitchen, thinking only of her bathtub and sleep.

On her bed is a pale-green box wrapped with a heavy black silk ribbon.

She knows who it's from and where it's from. She's wary, but she checks herself. It could be silk pajamas, a sweet gesture to his tired darling. He is attentive like that. She shouldn't be annoyed by a gift.

Inside is a black lace corset, stockings and a plastic hotel card key with a sticky note on it that reads *Ritz #1204*.

Of all nights, he chooses this one? They have been discussing this. Discussing his fantasies of being at her mercy, of being taken, not taking.

She is exhausted. He knows this. She hasn't had time for him all week, has been avoiding his calls, only answering in texts. He has likely been feeling her absence, which makes him want this more.

She has tried before, but she felt silly—last time she actually started laughing, which ended things early and hurt his feelings.

She lifts the corset out of the tissue paper, a beautiful and expensive item unlike anything she's ever worn. She feels pissy and put upon. How clueless can he be? There is no way she is driving downtown feeling so tired. She dumps the lace back in the box. She'll have to call and explain, make her apologies.

She walks into the bathroom to run water for her bath. She takes her skirt off, her blouse—in the mirror catching sight of the pale skin that's been sitting under fluorescent lights too long, the bluish circles under her eyes from too many late nights.

He'll be upset. Clearly he's put a lot of effort into this. Things at his job have been slower, and while this is a source of stress for him, it's given him time to plan. She envies him this space. She hasn't had time to think of anything outside work. But he has. And he wants what he wants. She wonders how long he will be content to keep asking her for it.

She thinks maybe she'll see if the corset fits, maybe she'll keep it and wear it for him another day when she's less tired.

It fits perfectly, lace hugging her waist, satin lifting her tits. She is impressed and flattered that he knows her body this well. And something about this is endearing, a bit exciting.

There are no panties in the box, a decided choice he's made, not an oversight—always the pervert. She rolls up the black stockings, fumbling as she clips them, unused to this apparatus.

For good measure, she slips into a pair of high black heels she already owns, the ones with the red soles.

Lingering in the bottom of the box is a riding crop. She picks it up gingerly. It's light and polished with a tight loop of leather at the end—a compelling accessory. Holding it, she looks in the mirror and is intrigued. She looks strong, powerful, a little obscene—her breasts, her sex, her ass on display, her waist tiny, the glossy elegant crop in her hand. For a brief instant she sees what he must imagine when he thinks of her like this.

She sees how he wants her.

She turns off the bath water and lets it drain.

She takes the white trench coat out of her closet to cover up and before she can rethink it, she grabs the key card off the bed and is downstairs and in her car.

Driving downtown past the lake, she tries to get her head in the proper space to do this for him, to him. She wants to be what he wants, what he needs. She is tired, yes, but shifting gears, driving through the night, bare except for his gift and her coat, she's getting excited. This time she vows she won't laugh. The riding crop on the seat next to her strengthens her decision.

Walking through the lobby, getting in the elevator, she tugs at her coat, constantly reminded of her secret, that she is walking exposed. The handle of the riding crop is jammed in an inside pocket, threatening to fall out. She presses it to her side.

She grows taller, more vibrant as she walks down the hall to the room. She can do this, she thinks.

She doesn't knock, but takes the key card out of her pocket and fishes the crop out of her jacket so it is in her hand. It gives her a feeling of command that surprises as it reassures. She looks down the empty hall; no one has seen her, and this further coaxes her into the mental space he has asked her to occupy.

He's slumped on the edge of the bed drinking a beer, watching sports on TV when she walks in. An empty bottle on the night table, yellow tie loose around his neck, shirt open at the first two buttons. She can see from his clenched hands, from the way he jumps up when she walks in, that he's wound tight. She wonders how long he's been waiting. His dark hair is a disheveled mess, like he's been pushing his hands through it while he's been waiting. He tries to flatten it down when he sees her looking at it. She wonders if he had decided she wasn't coming.

"I got your present," she says, walking into the room.

He says nothing, a relieved smile on his face as he places the beer on a table, clicks off the TV, but his eyes are questioning. She thinks she sees his hands tremble as he reaches for her. And that tremble sets off a small tremor in her chest—excitement and fear and desire.

She wants to set the tone immediately, let him know that tonight she is in charge. She brings the crop down on his bicep, and he immediately springs back.

"We need to have a little talk," she says, worried she's hit him too hard.

"I just," he starts, ready to explain, but she brings down the crop again on his other arm, this time trying to be softer.

"Quiet," she says, walking behind him. It's easier without him watching her, and the room feels intense already. However, he's craning his head toward her.

"Eyes front," she says, pushing his jaw with the handle of the crop. A little shudder runs through him as she mashes his cheek and that makes her smile. He's so eager for her like this; he finds pleasure in the smallest things, and this fuels her. She takes a moment to admire his well-formed shoulders, his hips narrower than hers.

"Now," she says, coming around to stand behind his shoulder where he can't see her so she can speak directly in his ear. "You left a present for me at my house. A present is something you give someone that you think would please *them*. Something they would enjoy. Maybe something that would soothe them after a long week of work. But you didn't really give me a present, did you?" This is surprisingly easy to say. It's how she truly feels.

He hesitates and swallows. She notices the goose bumps on his neck—her encouragement. "No," he says.

"No. Your present is a demand. Getting this room, making me come down here to you, it's all about you. Isn't it?" She feels herself slipping into this role—fueled by his response, fueled by her week of being diplomatic and strategic and at service to others' whims, fueled by his desire for honesty and for her to be in control now.

"Yes," he says, quietly.

"What would you say if I told you I thought that was pretty selfish?"

He's silent at that.

She's moving farther into the mental space that he has asked her to occupy, becoming who he has told her he needs. Though she would never want to actually hurt him, he has given her the crop for a reason. She swats his ass. "I asked a question."

He drops his eyes and turns toward her. "I'd say you're probably right. Look, sweetheart, I'm sorry, I didn't think..."

"Eyes front," she says, smiling now. "I don't want apologies. I want you to make it up to me." She walks around and stands in front of him and in a low voice says, "I'm not your sweetheart. Kneel."

She tries not to smile at how quickly he complies, his eyes alight with excitement and gratitude. "I would punish you for being so bratty," she says. "But I think that would only please you, wouldn't it?"

"Yes," he admits, softly.

"So I think instead, you'll be at my mercy tonight to please me. Undress."

She bites the inside of her cheek to hide her smile at his eager scrambling. He rises to take off his shirt, pants and boxers and then he is kneeling at her feet, naked and beautiful and already hard.

She sits down on the edge of the bed, crossing her legs demurely so he can see nothing, and plants a shoe in his face. "Massage," she says.

If this is what he wants, then tonight she's going to give it to him all the way. She knows he loves her feet.

He removes her shoe, and she guides his large hands up under her coat to the clasps of her stockings. He unsnaps them, his hands gentle and slow on her thighs as he rolls the stockings down her legs. Then his strong fingers are on her foot, working her arch, the ball, her heel.

She leans her head back, eyes closed.

He's thorough; he always is. Before she's lulled into complete relaxation she says, "Enough."

He places an adoring, open-mouthed kiss on the top of her foot, eyes intense.

She uncrosses her legs then, still in her trench, not wanting to show him that she has complied with his unspoken demands and worn the corset. But as she uncrosses and recrosses her legs, she shows him that she is bare underneath. She hears his breath catch.

She puts the other shoe near his face, and he complies—taking it off, then her stockings, massaging her foot until her shoulders lower and her body feels warm. She's read somewhere that all the pressure points of the body correspond to pressure points in the foot, and tonight she believes it.

"Kiss," she says, and he kisses her foot.

She looks down at his erection so hard it bounces off his stomach. She stands and pads over to the window with her back to him. He's still on his knees. It must be getting uncomfortable for him. She is fumbling with what to do next and glad he can't see her face. She needs a moment to plot out how to proceed, if she can proceed. She has to think the steps through. The look in his eye gives her confidence—adoration and desire and desperation. He only wants to be used. And he is so turned on, attentive to every move she makes and direction she gives. "Stand," she says, walking to him. "Take off my coat."

He fumbles with the buckle, his hands shaking slightly, but he gets it, and the buttons, and then reveals her in his offering. She's sure he's about to say something. She waits, her crop poised to correct him if he speaks.

But he turns and actually hangs up her coat in the closet. She wants to laugh, tries not to smile. He is usually messy, leaving things everywhere. It's a bone of contention between them. Tonight he is taking his role seriously.

She can't help but lean forward and kiss him, wondering if kissing is allowed, if it is what a good dominatrix would do.

Hot and open, her tongue is immediately in his mouth, claiming, demanding. When she pulls back his eyes are glazed with lust.

"Sit," she says. And he sits on the edge of the bed.

"On the floor," she says. And he is immediately down, sitting with his back to the bed, his legs out in front of him.

She reaches down, threading her fingers in the thick hair at the back of his head, gripping as she places her feet on either side of his hips. This huge man—six feet and some, strong and proud—is willingly at her feet. She feels a rush of power as he looks up at her, eyes filled with desire and hope. "Open," she says, as she places her sex at his mouth.

She can feel his enthusiasm in the first touch of his tongue—a hard lick from the bottom to the top where he sucks her clit in his mouth and lightly tongues it just how she likes.

"Fuck, I love your mouth." She can feel him smile against her.

His head is between her thighs, caught between her and the edge of the bed as she grips his hair, hard. His tongue is heaven. For a brief moment she thinks he is making shapes against her, is spelling something in tight circles, and then his hand comes up, two fingers slipping inside. And it's bliss.

She should stop him. She didn't tell him he could touch her. But he feels amazing, and she's close.

Next time, she thinks, next time she'll bind his hands.

And the thought of him sitting with his hands bound behind his back, in her mind she's added a blindfold as well, at her mercy while he licks her, is enough to push her over the edge and she comes—white light and obliteration, shaking thighs and raising on tiptoe.

She steps back and he's panting, hair mussed; the look in his eyes—she has never felt more powerful or adored, never more loved.

"I know what you need," she says, as she rubs his head where she gripped his hair.

He is almost pitiful as he collapses at her feet, kissing her toes. With his mouth against her ankles he is whispering, thanking her.

"Up," she says, taking her crop from the floor where it has fallen and prodding his ribs. She knows what he wants now. To be ordered, to be taken, to know that he is loved.

She turns him so he's facing the bed. She rips off the blankets down to the sheets and reaches up to whisper in his ear. "Bend over."

He hesitates and she swats his ass with the crop. She's figured out the right velocity, the correct pressure.

"No stalling," she says. "Chest on the bed."

He leans over, ass in the air, face in the sheets.

She takes his hands and places them behind his back. "Don't move them," she says.

She trails her crop down his back and with the handle she nudges his legs apart. They're tense, and he's clenched. There is something thrilling about coming up right next to his limit. And she is more than curious as to what he would allow her to do to him, when he would stop her.

But now that she has him in this position, she's unsure of how far to push. She walks around the edge of the bed. He looks good—back flexed, mouth open. He's watching her, one side of his face pressed to the sheets—both dazed and seriously intent.

"Should I leave you like I found you?" she asks. "Perhaps I should head home and get a good night's sleep." She'll do no such thing. He knows it too. But she must be somewhat convincing because he looks panicked. "That's what it means when I'm in charge."

His eyes are on her bare sex as she walks back behind him contemplating her next move and his perfect ass.

"Spread," she says.

He doesn't move.

"Again with the stalling." She smacks the back of his legs.

He opens shoulder width.

She reaches under him and skims her hand over his balls, making him jump, and then drags her fingers up between his cheeks. "Anyone ever touched you here?"

"No," he says quietly.

She's tracing him now with her crop handle. "So I'm the only one." He's starting to squirm. She can see his pulse beating in his neck. Since she's never done something like this, she isn't going to stick the crop handle up his ass. She wants him to feel out of control, in her control, and they are rubbing up against the edge of it. He's uncomfortable and yet still there with her, surrendering to her, and for tonight that is probably enough to get him where he wants to go.

His eyes follow her as she climbs past him up on the bed and settles against the pillows at the top, legs open, giving him a stellar view of her pussy.

"Now," she says. "As you know, I had a long exhausting week, didn't I?"

"Yes," he says.

"So I think it only fair that you service me," she says. His chest is off the bed immediately, and he's standing. She actually laughs. "Now, there's no hesitation."

He smiles at that, standing at the foot of the bed.

"Come," she says, reaching out for him. "Show me how much you want to please me."

He practically leaps on top of her, hovering, his weight on both elbows. No part of him touches her except his hard cock and she pauses under him looking at the lean planes of his chest, his stomach, everything at attention. The lush delight of having this man under her control overwhelms and surprises her. She thinks she understands now the rush, the power that comes from demanding exactly what you want *and* from being your lover's heart's desire. His arms start to tremble, and this brings her back to him, to his fantasy.

She reaches her crop around his back. "You don't come until I say so." He stifles a moan and she flicks the crop on his flank. "Understand?"

He nods.

She reaches down with her free hand, grasping him and

bringing him to her, then she rolls her hips up, taking him inside, feeling him fill her.

He groans.

"Quiet," she says, and flicks her crop against his ass. She reaches up to his ear. "Or I'll deny you." And she plants a kiss on his neck as he collapses on top of her.

She flicks his ass with her crop and sets a rhythm and time for his thrusts. Starting him slow and deep, her eyes close and she almost drops the crop, he feels so good inside her.

She can feel the quiver in his legs. He's not going to last long as worked up as he is. And she wants it to be good for him, wants this to be a successful night.

She speeds him, flicking him with the crop faster and he is eager to please. She can feel herself getting closer to her own edge—his cock filling her, the enthusiasm in each thrust. Already his head is thrown back, and she knows he's thinking of something to hold off his own climax—baseball stats or the track list for Physical Graffiti, something besides her, something outside of this moment. She doesn't want him anywhere but here. Even if he comes before she gets hers.

She reaches up and pulls his face to hers. "Now," she says in his open mouth. Then she snakes her hand down between them.

He becomes impossibly harder, his thrusts erratic and needy, and the look on his face is intense as he leans his forehead against hers and mouths the word he has never allowed himself to say before, the word he has always wanted to say, "Mistress." Watching him, she falls over the edge again, overwhelming but sweeter, a release and a union as he too climaxes.

His arms stayed locked around her, even after she's slipped him out and he's rolled to his side and they're lying in a wet mess. He's buried his face in her shoulder, kissing, his hands roaming the lace at her waist, devoted and adoring.

But she's nervous now, exposed and insecure. She liked it, more than she thought she would. She hopes it was enough, that she is enough.

"You feel okay?" she asks.

"I feel delirious," he says, smiling against her shoulder. "And more in love than I thought I could be," he says, looking up and kissing her mouth sweetly.

Then he takes the crop from her hands and drops it on the floor next to the bed.

# MATES

Jillian Boyd

"Ask me how my date went."

I nearly jumped in shock as Sam sat down opposite me. I hadn't heard him coming—I was too busy studying for my evening-school class. Sam's face smacked of irritation and winter cold. He would have looked cute if he hadn't been twitching.

"It was shit, Lara. Probably the worst date of my entire adult life," he said, not giving me the chance to ask about it first.

I sipped my coffee, rolling my eyes. "You said that the last time too."

"Yes, but this time, it was. Terrible, and humiliating too."

"It can't have been worse than the time your trousers fell down."

"I accidentally called her 'mum' in front of her polo mates."

"Jesus. What happened there?"

"They were making me nervous! They were all posh, Oxbridge-type blokes, yammering about their cars. You know what I get like when I'm nervous!"

I resisted bringing up the incident with the fishmonger and the old lady at Harrods...

"What was she doing bringing her mates to a date anyway?"

"She said she needed a chaperone. She didn't mention there'd be five of them."

"I could have gone along. I can take on a bunch of Oxbridge louts without breaking a sweat."

"Lara, you know what it's like when I take you anywhere. They think we're on a date, and they ask questions, and you get nervous and break out in hives."

I couldn't contest that, so I switched the subject and asked Sam if I could get him tea. As a diversion tactic, tea never failed. When I tottered back to the table, trying to balance two cups of Earl Grey, Sam was leafing through my book.

"I have never seen the word *cunt* used so many times in an academic text."

"It's a text on etymology and the language of sexuality." I said, handing him his tea. "I'm trying to read it for my linguistics class."

"Trying to?"

"It's a lot of words."

Sam smirked as he sugared up his brew. Two sugars, splash of milk, as he'd done since we met. He was comfortingly predictable.

"Valentine's Day is coming up." I said, stirring sweetener into my tea. "Sod's law that I haven't got a date. Again."

"And how have you not got blokes lining up down the road for the pleasure of spending Valentine's Day with you?"

"Oh, come on. You know the types of blokes I attract. Either they're hiding some disgusting character trait at first or they're disappointed I'm not actually a supermodel."

"You've done modeling though."

"Yeah, life modeling for an art class. It's not like I'm stomping it out on the catwalk at London Fashion Week, is it?"

"It's still modeling, Lara. If the fact that you're not on the cover of *Vogue* every month puts them off, fuck them."

"I'd rather not, thanks."

Sam snorted, stirring more sugar in his tea. "Valentine's Day. It's shit anyway. Cupids and chocolates and love hearts."

"Naughty lingerie, champagne, candles, the promise of kinky sex later in the evening..."

I sighed wistfully. Sam's eyes glazed over for a moment, as if he was remembering something naughty himself. And then he grinned in that way he did when he had an idea that couldn't possibly go right.

"How about we celebrate Valentine's Day together?"

I blinked. "What?"

"Well, we're both single, we're best friends and we know what we both like. Why not? Like a mate's agreement."

"See, I always thought a mate's agreement was something like us agreeing to get married if we're alone by the time we're forty."

"Yeah, but this one happens faster. Come on, Lara. It'll be fun!"

"Really, though? Because not twenty minutes ago you were telling me that it's awkward taking me places! With the questions and the sweating and the hives, remember?"

"It'll just be us. I'll set it up, and you just have to come. Nothing embarrassing. Promise."

I thought about it. I studied his face, trying to see if he wasn't about to burst into laughter and tell me it was a joke. But he didn't waver. Eventually, with a sigh, I nodded.

"All right. But we're not going to shag, are we?"

He shook his head, a bit too wildly. "No, no. No shagging."

"Because that would be awkward."

"Yes...it would be."

But there was something in his eyes, something that told me that he might not have been entirely averse to the idea. It made me feel a bit off-kilter. The thought of any sex with Sam was a bit too much for the afternoon.

Nevertheless, it stuck with me, even later that day during class. As I listened to our tutor icily droning on about synonyms for *vagina*, in that frosty lecture hall, little fantasies about feeling Sam's naked body close to mine, about being caught in a spiral of ecstasy, were the only thing keeping me warm...

That and the two big woolly sweaters I was wearing.

The next day, I tried not to think about anything relating to Sam, Valentine's Day and shagging. Well, tried to. I did all right until just before lunchtime, when my phone pinged with a message.

*Are you more of a Brad Pitt kind of girl, or Tom Cruise?*

*x S*

I blinked, trying to figure out what that meant. The penny took a little too long to drop.

*Have you not been to the cinema since the nineties? Neither, thanks. Why?*

*L*

I grabbed my wallet and went toward the cafeteria. My friend Betsy, from IT, was waiting at the elevator.

"Thank god for lunch," she said, retying her ponytail. "Seven calls from Mr. James from HR today."

"Jesus. What was it this time?"

"The same old bullshit spiel about his laptop not turning on properly. If I need to keep reminding the head of HR of a big tech company to plug his fucking laptop in..."

"Is he still calling you Busty?"

"No, thank god. We've progressed to *Bunty*."

"Well…it's something." I said. Betsy sighed, deeply. The lift pinged, at the same time as my phone.

*I wanted to know what film to get for our date. Or if you wanted a film at all. I could just rent some porn and we'll have a laugh.*

*Oh my god, ignore that last bit. Fuck!*

*x S*

I read the text again, feeling my face flush. Or was it the heating in the lift? Either way, I switched back into midday natter with Betsy. The cafeteria was surprisingly empty for a Wednesday, which made my incoming text alert sound like it was echoing off the walls.

*You said something about sexy knickers?*

*x S*

I nearly let my phone clatter into my bowl of soup.

"You all right?" asked Betsy, before gingerly dipping her spoon into the chicken broth. Well, at least that's what it said on the menu. "Only, you're looking a bit…nervous."

"Me? Nervous? No, no, not at all. Just a long day, is all."

The phone pinged again. And again. My face felt hotter than the broth was.

*What's your bra size? I want to get you something fancy.*

*x S*

*Fuck, this is awkward. I'm at Agent Provocateur and it feels like I'm drowning in lace.*

*x S*

"Every time you get a text, you look like you're going to jump through the roof. What's up?"

"Nothing, nothing at all!"

Betsy narrowed her eyes. "Are you sexting with someone?"

she asked, barely able to repress a giggle.

"I'm not...sexting with someone. Keep your voice down!"

As if I wasn't embarrassed enough, another text came in.

*HELP! I DON'T KNOW BRAS!*

*x S*

I quickly typed in a reply, to the sound of Betsy's now full-on giggle.

*You don't have to buy me a bra! I've got hundreds of them!*

*L*

"Come on, Lara. Spill the beans."

I sighed. "It's just Sam."

"You're sexting with Sam?"

"No, I'm not bloody sexting with Sam! It's just that...I may have agreed to do something silly and now he keeps reminding me of it."

"Silly, as in a bet?"

"Silly as in...I agreed to spend Valentine's Day with him. As mates."

Betsy raised her eyebrows in surprise. "You've agreed to spend Valentine's Day with Sam...as mates."

"Yes! Do I need to draw a diagram? It's just an agreement between friends, is all."

"Well, from the way you're blushing and jumping at every beep of your phone, I'd say it's not just a mates' agreement."

"What are you suggesting?"

Betsy groaned dramatically. "Oh, come on. You and Sam. With all the history. And this is Sam's idea. Connect the dots, *mate*!"

"Bets, I've known Sam for long enough that I can trust him to not make this into anything more than what it is. He's my best friend, and we're just going to have a lovely day together."

"Sure you are, Lara, a lovely day followed by eight hours of wall-to-wall shagging. Just remember to hydrate."

I rolled my eyes, as another text pinged up.

*Having a sit down at Pret. Not going into Lace War Zone again. Got you fluffy pajamas.*

*x S*

Sam and I had been inseparable for nearly ten years now. We met when I was twenty-one, freshly dumped by an absolute tosspot. In a fit of heartbroken pique, I went to a bar to get absolutely blind drunk and fuck the first thing in sight. The first thing in sight just happened to be Sam Moran. He had a side job as a barman and as I stumbled up to him, cheeks stained with running mascara, he looked concerned. Or possibly terrified.

"I need the strongest booze you've got," I said, trying to come over bold as brass but ending up a bit south of vexed kitten.

Sam sized me up. "Are you sure it's booze you want?"

"Well, I've just been dumped by the love of my life, and I'm in a shitty dive bar in Brixton at one in the morning, looking like the lost member of KISS. So, yeah, booze me up."

"Right. I'll see what I can do for you."

He rumbled around on the shelves and produced a bottle of something I'd never even seen before. Mind you, I wasn't exactly down with the alcohol back then, so it could have just been vodka. But for whatever reason, I was trying to sound a bit harder than I felt.

"Is this the strongest you've got?" I said, my voice a wobbly mess between cold and hard and "please give me a hug."

"Well, I don't know, ma'am," he drawled, his voice a thick, honeyed layer of Western gunslinger. I'm just a humble temp trying to keep up my equally humble student wages."

"Fuck off, Cowboy Slim."

"Actually, it's Sam. And for what it's worth, any guy who

makes you feel this shitty is not even fit to put a pinkie on your quiver, let alone be the love of your life."

"A pinkie on my quiver? What kind of a euphemism is that?"

"Archery. A quiver is what you keep your arrows in. Ah, never mind. You get my point, right?"

My determination to get drunk wavered and I couldn't keep myself from laughing. He was possibly the most awkward person I'd ever met, but there was something about him that made me feel...well, okay about myself.

"Now, that's a bloody good laugh. Dirty as fuck," Sam said, as he poured me a Coke.

"As am I," I said, before I could hold myself back. I covered my mouth in embarrassment. "Oops. Lara. That's my name."

"Nice to meet you, Oops Lara."

I didn't end up on top of him that night. But if you think about it, it was only natural that we became inseparable. We talked about everything that night, from our hatred for queuing and our shared love of Paul McGann's Eighth Doctor. Soon, we were holding hands, giggling over private jokes and cuddling up. And if you think about that, it was only natural that people started asking questions. But we were mates, honestly. Platonic best mates...

And now we were spending Valentine's Day together. Thinking about it, it was a mystery as to why we hadn't before. Plenty were the times when both of us were single, alone and bored off our skulls on that day.

Valentine's was everywhere. Even as I sat down for lunch in our favorite café, all I saw were couples. Coupling all over the place, walking down Oxford Street, hand in hand, arm in arm, occasionally stealing loving glances at each other.

There were hundreds of other people about, of course, but my eyes kept being drawn to couples. And the occasional solo flyer, loaded with bags.

The tall, bespectacled ginger bloke carrying the H. Samuels bag…he would be proposing tonight. Maybe over a dinner at the place they first met. Girl with the blonde hair coming out of the sex shop across the road…maybe a nice corset and a pair of frilly knickers…or a whip and some handcuffs.

I sighed, that weird feeling settling in my chest again. This time, I was sure it was butterflies—partly nerves, mostly a deep longing to hear Sam's voice, telling me silly stuff. Telling me he…I don't know. I got out my phone and called him.

"Lara?" he answered, sounding surprised. " Are you sneaking in calls during work hours again, you cheeky girl?"

"That was once, and it was to my mum! Anyway…I just wanted to see if you'd planned anything massive for our celebration tomorrow. You know, so I can adequately prepare and primp."

He chuckled, a bit nervously. "Don't worry. It's just going to be at my flat. The two of us, some curry and *Die Hard* on Netflix or something. Nothing surprising. No primping required."

My heart sank deep into my pumps. "Oh, right."

"You sound almost disappointed."

"Oh no. *Die Hard* and a curry. Wonderful. Proper mates stuff. I say, what's all that noise in the background? Are you not at work?"

"I'm just out getting something for a colleague's leaving do. You know, flowers, something special, and that."

"Right. Something special. Sounds top tip."

"I've got to go. Bloody queue isn't moving. Remember, my flat, tomorrow at eight."

"Tomorrow at mate…um, eight! Right, bye!"

As I quickly ended the call, I suddenly felt less keen on my sandwich and more so on mauling a tub of ice cream. I should have been okay with the idea. No surprises, no sudden romantic confessions. Film and curry.

Just mates. Nothing more.

"Happy Cupid Day!"

Betsy sashayed into my office, and deposited a big heart-shaped box on my desk. "It's the fancy stuff."

"Aw, you lifesaver! I'm having a bitch of a day so far. Thank you. Sit down. Have a cuppa with me. Or, you know, five."

"Thank god. I could use a break," she said, pulling up a chair and delving into the chocolates. "So, how are the preparations for Definitely Platonic Valentine's Evening going? Is Boots out of condoms yet?"

"We're not going to shag! And don't ask. Really. It's quite bad."

"What's Brothario got planned for you, then?"

"One, that's a terrible, terrible word. And two...well, nothing special. Genuinely nothing special."

"Define nothing special?"

"A night of curries and Netflix. That's it."

Betsy blinked. "That's...that's really it?"

"Yes. For Valentine's Day, we're eating Tandoori and watching *Die Hard*. Like he said, just something between mates."

Betsy raised an eyebrow. She looked like she was mulling over the idea, making faces and noises as she went along. It started to irritate me.

"What? What are you thinking?"

"Well, he's obviously lying his face off, because he fancies you and tonight's the night he's going to tell you."

I snorted. "Right. And you know this how?"

"Oh, come on, Lara! Think it through. Think it through very thoroughly, and don't give me that spiel about men and women and being just friends. This is not that sort of situation."

"This is also not a Richard Curtis film!"

"Why must you be so cynical? Open your heart, and let Valentine's Day magic blah blah blah! Oh, I must say, I do pick out some quality chocolate."

Betsy punctuated the sentence with another bite from a truffle. "I mean, if I can get a date on Valentine's, surely that's proof that magic happens on days like this."

I raised my eyebrows. "It's not the guy from HR, is it?"

"Christ, no. He's...actually, he's also a friend of mine. He's been living abroad and now he's back in town and wants to take me out."

"Good stuff. Are you going to buy him chocolate as well?"

"If it gets me into his pants, I'll fucking buy him a chocolate fountain. Seriously, Lara. Even if you don't want to see what's obviously there, Sam might...no, *will* surprise you. Mark my wise words."

"Consider them marked," I said, grabbing for another chocolate but then realizing we'd eaten them all. Betsy and I looked at each other in dismay. "Well...it's a better lunch than the chicken soup in the cafeteria today," I eventually said, sighing. Curry and Netflix was actually starting to sound like a sensible idea, god help me.

"Sam, I'm running ridiculously late, but I'm on my way to your flat now. I'm just leaving the station...shit, it's pissing down outside. God, you better have the heating on. See you in a minute."

Sam wasn't answering his phone, and I had no desire to keep trying until he did, so I left a message while trying to navigate the February drench without an umbrella. Luckily, he didn't live too far away from Marylebone Station. Still, as I made my way through the amber-lit streets, past the antique market, it felt like forever. By now, I just wanted to be warm and fed. It didn't matter what he'd planned.

"He might surprise you..." Who was Betsy kidding? All I needed now from Sam was his own brand of comfortable predictability. And as I pressed his buzzer and opened the heavy iron doors to the building, I'd almost convinced myself of just that.

The neon lights buzzed, like a soundtrack to me going up the stairs and toward his flat. The door was slightly ajar, but I knocked anyway—lord knows I was comfortably predictable myself.

"Sam, I'm so terribly sorry, but work and clients and...holy shit."

Surprise me he had. It was dark in his flat, save for what must have been hundreds of tiny candles, coloring the place in an ethereal glow. There was D'Angelo playing on the stereo, and my nostrils were tickled by the unmistakable scent of cake.

And Sam, there he was. Standing there, looking a bit guilty, with his hands in his pockets.

"So, no curry and Bruce Willis, then?" I said, after just about managing to pick my jaw up from the floor.

He shook his head. "Not really, no. There's cake though."

"There's cake. You made cake."

"Yeah. You like cake."

"And there's D'Angelo on the stereo. And candles everywhere."

"Yeah...that's not everything, mind."

He dug into his pockets and produced a velvet-lined box, the sight of which made me panic. Sam spotted it and laughed nervously. "It's just earrings. Got them at Selfridges."

Shaped like a teardrop, a little blue sparkle… "So, that wasn't a leaving present for your workmate, then."

"I fibbed. Sorry. I've also got you pink roses."

"Right. I'm sorry, I'm just a bit flabbergasted. And nervous."

"Don't worry. Fuck knows, I'm nervous too. I want to tell you something, but I don't really know how to say it without sounding like a massive fool, and I'm afraid that if I tell you and you don't like it, you'll walk out that door and out of my life, and I can't bear the thought of losing you."

He swallowed, trembling. I knew exactly what it was, and I didn't know what to do. Sam. Cowboy Slim. My best mate. All those whispers, all those "When are you two getting married?" comments…

"Then don't say it," I said, crossing the floor of his flat and taking his hand in mine. "Show it to me."

There was a beat. Two beats. I could practically feel him shaking like a leaf in a storm. I didn't realize. Why didn't I realize? And why were my lips, after all this denial, practically screaming for his? He was trying to say it, I knew he was. His mouth stuck on the word "I" for longer than eternity. The silence was deafening.

So I took control. I answered the question he didn't ask with my lips, the brush of my mouth against his. He whimpered, but took hold of himself and replied by claiming my lips, kissing me with a hungry force. I let myself melt into him, his frame harder and more muscular than I'd ever realized.

The kiss lasted what felt like eternity, only lit by the glow of the sea of candles. When he pulled away, my lips were still puckering, wanting—no, needing—more.

"So…that," he said, his breath heavy. "Well no, not just that."

"There's more?"

"There's also this."

He grabbed me by the collar of my shirt and kissed me again: this time, fully in control. His mouth tasted, kissed and tasted again, sliding his lips along my jaw and leaving a hard mark on my neck that would no doubt be purple come the morning. He nipped his way up to my ear.

"Please tell me there's more." I whimpered, my pussy quivering with liquid lust.

"God, so much more," he answered, before he took my hand and dragged me toward his bedroom, like he was dragging me into the unknown.

Sam's hands were softer than I remembered them to be. Free of the guitar string-induced calluses he once boasted, they roamed the expanse of my naked body, mapping out every inch of me like a carnal cartographer, taking their time. His lips were able assistants, kissing, sucking and nibbling their way around.

It was only when his hands reached my mound that he seemed to falter. He looked down at me, his eyes questioning and wanting.

"Can I...please..." he stammered, as if he wanted to shred that last niggling fear of crossing this boundary. My answer was to grab his hand and take it where it wanted to go. He let out a moan as his fingers danced across my pussy lips, finding my plump clit.

"God, Lara, you feel so wet. So amazing."

His fingers circled around my little bud, only briefly, but effectively. I felt a little shock of ecstatic static running through me, making me moan.

Sam pulled back, briefly taken aback, which made me giggle. "It's okay," I said. "Feels good. I've not been touched like that in a long while."

"Touched like what?" said Sam, continuing his circles.

"Like...like I mean something. With adoration," I managed, before my breath hitched.

"Oh, Lara," he said, pulling his hand away—to my dismay—and blazing a path of kisses from my neck, down my tummy. "Every inch of you is made to be adored. God, I just want to...I just want to...I just want you."

Another ragged breath escaped my lips, as his mouth lingered dangerously close to exactly where I wanted it to be.

"Please tell me what you want me to do."

I could feel his hot breath against the wetness of my labia. My heart pounded in my throat and my head swam. It was like flipping the final switch. What did I want? What did *I* want?

"Everything."

"Are you absolutely sure?" Sam asked, looking into my eyes for reassurance. I nodded.

"Yes. Everything. Now."

"Everything. Now," he repeated, breathing in deeply to center himself. "Oh, Miss Lara Rhodes. I'll give you everything you want and more. Now."

With that, he took hold of my legs and spread me open, dipping his head between my thighs and letting his mouth feast on my wet pussy. His tongue lapped messily at my clit, which caused me to dig my heels into his back and grab a tuft of his hair.

Supine beneath him, with my legs crossed over his muscular back, I writhed as he gently but effectively sucked my clit, his fingers joining and stroking my plump wetness. I felt my body flush with a red-hot lust, and just when I thought I couldn't handle anything more, he slid his fingers inside me, making me cry out.

"Tell me when I've hit the spot," he said, circling and probing in search of that one sweet spot that would sure enough be my undoing

"Oh god, you shouldn't," I gasped. "Sam, it'll be messy, and... Oh, Christ, right there."

"Right...here, you say?"

His fingers curled into my G-spot, driving back and forth with increasing pressure. "Yes, right there! Oh...oh, sweet lord," I panted, as his tongue and fingers worked as one. My hips bucked to meet with his movements, going ever harder and faster.

I could feel something inside me changing, from a spongy tenderness to a tight knot, and I knew what would happen even before my inner walls tightened to grip his fingers. Then I felt myself melt into climax, my juices sloppily cascading onto my thighs, Sam's face and his sheets. I let out a wail, as I shuddered out my orgasm clutching onto the sheets.

I landed back on Earth to find Sam looking at me, eyes wide open and mouth shining with my juices. His mouth formed a perfect *O*, and his hand was instinctively wrapped around his hard, beautiful cock. My pussy twitched with greedy longing.

"Are you okay?" he asked, absentmindedly stroking himself.

I nodded, licking my lips. "Sam...please," I said, letting my legs fall open. "Please."

"Do you want me inside you?"

"Yes."

"Do you want to make love?"

My arms flailed at him, trying to pull him on top of me, but he wouldn't have it just yet. He wanted to hear me say it.

"Do you want us...do you want me to make love to you?"

"Yes."

"Say it again."

"Yes!"

"Say it again!"

"Yes, Sam, please make love to me and do it bloody quickly because I might actually explode!"

"Sorry," he said, crawling on top of me, his eyes dark with lusty fire. "I wanted to make sure I wasn't dreaming."

It did feel like dreaming. One fiery fever dream, as he positioned the head of his cock against my opening and sank himself deep inside me. A shuddering breath escaped him, along with a whispered, "Thank you." His cock felt big and hefty inside me, filling me up like it was always meant to be that way. I gasped, my body anticipating the thrust.

But he lingered there, his lips hovering above mine, waiting as if he wanted to etch this moment in his memories forever. I let out a moan, before he covered my lips with his, grabbed my hand and made his move.

Together, we rocked steadily, with Sam building up a hypnotizing rhythm. I grabbed on to his hips, feeling the flow of them, letting my hands cup his firm buttocks.

"You feel so good," he breathed, before shifting so I could feel the friction of his pubic bone against my swollen clit. He cursed, grinding hard against me. I could feel a dizzy heat spiraling through my pussy, up to my lower belly. God, the way he moved made me light-headed. I clawed at his back as he sped up. He brought me close, so tantalizingly close…just a few more thrusts, just a few more.

And then he retreated. I blinked rapidly, confused. "What? What's wrong?"

But without any words, he positioned me on my hands and knees, entering me again and whispering "I want to make you come," before his hand reached around to circle my clit. His thrusts were rough, almost erratic, but his fingers were steady and fast, getting me right there again.

"So close, so close," I slurred.

"Come for me, Lara. Come hard," he said, driving himself into me. It took him four more thrusts before I felt myself erupting from the center of my body, pleasure clouding all my senses. I rode out my climax as I let him take his. With a deep, guttural crying out of my name, he grabbed my hips with a near-bruising strength, shuddering into me.

And then he finally said the words he'd been dying to say.

"I love you so much, Lara."

I collapsed forward onto the bed, he curling up against me. To my surprise, tears stung in my eyes. But I smiled, as his warmth surrounded me.

"You don't have to say it back if you can't yet. Or, ever, you know. If you just want to..."

"Sam. I want to. It's there, deep in my heart. Just give me time. Let's...let's see where this goes."

He smiled, looking relieved. "Go with the flow?"

"Something like that, yeah. Hey, Cowboy Slim...what was this about you baking a cake? I could go for a piece right now. And a massive drink."

"Postcoital cake eating. I like that. Don't move. I'll get everything you need."

Sam stood up and walked toward the kitchen, giving me a glorious view of his moonlit backside.

"Cute ass," I giggled.

He turned around and shot me a wink. "Why, thank you, ma'am. I aim to please," he drawled.

*I could get used to this,* I thought, smiling. It wasn't awkward at all. In fact, it felt oddly right.

# CHAMPION

Kathleen Tudor

The humidity closed in around me, choking me as I struggled for breath. Sweat that had nothing to do with the heat stung my eyes and I blinked it away, not willing to risk lowering my guard for a second. I studied my opponent, crouching across the circle, her stance balanced and light. She was quick, but I had more reach and maybe a bit more muscle. Maybe.

She threw a punch from the left and I blocked it as contemptuously as she had thrown it, shaking off the testing jab without a thought. My world had narrowed to her body and its subtle shifts, feints, and tells. I knew an instant before her leg flew that she was going to kick, and moved quickly, striking back as one hand dropped to block her body shot, the other lifting to catch the "two" of her one-two combo next to my ear.

She turned it into a one-two-three before I could adjust, her third kick coming back in just under the hand I was already lifting to standard guard, and while I felt my own kicks land on the sharp hardness of arm bones, hers connected with my ribs. We both stepped back, circling once again, but from the corner of my eye I saw the flicker of the scoreboard changing. Her point.

I was getting frustrated, which was a mistake. This was the final round and that point put her firmly ahead. I bit down on my guard and struggled to clear my mind, my coach breaking into my thoughts from the sideline. "Thirty seconds, Riley!"

I breathed out, pushing the stress and the knowledge of my dwindling time out of the front of my mind, drawing myself slowly back into that place of pure awareness. And then I saw it. Her shift was subtle as she twisted, one foot going flat, eyes narrowing on mine, and I knew that she was going to turn to throw a back kick with the hopes of catching me by surprise and perhaps even knocking me down, draining away my precious few final seconds.

I was in motion as soon as she committed, my leg coming up with blinding force and power as she rotated, taking her eyes off me for just a second. It was a second too long. I was not where she expected me to be, and she spun right into my kick, my instep connecting with the side of her head just beside her temple. She went down hard, and I danced back, waiting for her to get up and give me an opportunity to take the final point.

A second later, I realized I'd already taken it. The ref lifted his left hand—the one on my side of the ring—and cheers erupted through the convention center, nearly drowning out the announcer as he called my name and division, but it was the two small words that followed that brought tears to my eyes: National Champion.

The woman coming to under the careful eyes of the on-site medical personnel would get the silver, and I, somehow, had taken gold. I glanced around, looking for some confirmation that I wasn't dreaming, and my coach slammed into me, his huge hands stinging as he patted my back with excessive force, uncaring that my gear was slick with my sweat. Then he spun me around and I walked to the center of the ring, facing my opponent, who had gotten shakily to her feet. She nodded. We bowed.

The adult black-belt divisions were held last, and so there were many fewer spectators now than there had been at opening. Still, it seemed like an endless parade of humanity as people congratulated me, posed me for pictures, and directed me through the medal ceremony. My teammates had all stayed—even those whose matches were long since done—to cheer for me and the few other people still awaiting their matches, and they grabbed me, squeezing me in hugs and tugging on the medal in playful, delighted congratulations.

Finally, back in the stands, team greeted, I was able to approach the one person I'd most looked forward to reaching. "Did you see it?"

My sweet, gentle husband grabbed me by the front of my sweaty gi and pulled me close, his lips capturing mine in a kiss that would have made me flush to my toes if I hadn't still been pinked from exertion. "You kicked her *ass*," he murmured.

I burst out laughing. "No, that would have been illegal. I guess you missed the fight…I kicked her in the *head*."

"My mistake," he said, eyes twinkling. We'd enrolled in Tae Kwon Do at the same time, thinking it would be a bonding activity, but he'd quickly dropped out when he'd realized that he couldn't bring himself to actually hit another person. That didn't make him any less supportive of *me* hitting people.

"I'll forgive you anything if there's food." Other than protein bars and water, none of us ate before matches for fear of sluggish limbs or, worse, vomiting in the ring.

With a magician's flourish, he produced a container of pasta salad with chicken. "You just love me for the food," he pretended to complain.

I was already too busy chewing to argue, and I also didn't resist as he pulled me gently toward a clear seat. He eased me down in between bites, and then sat down on the filthy stadium floor at my feet. I swallowed, meaning to protest, but his hand had crept up the leg of my gi pants and his fingers closed firmly around the muscles of my calf. A couple of teammates glanced over as I moaned, but they only smiled and went back to their conversations as James teased my calf muscles toward relaxation.

"You didn't stretch," he accused.

"I wanted to come find you," I said, not quite lying.

"Uh-huh." He squeezed a little harder and I stifled a yelp as he kneaded the knot away.

By the time our last two competitors had finished, one going home with a silver and the other with nothing more than a black eye, the pasta was gone and I was limp under my husband's hands.

Darryl accepted our sympathies politely, vanishing back to his hotel soon after, and Fiona came up last, jubilant at having medaled in the senior divisions. We hugged her and clapped her back, and soon everyone was gathering their things, chattering about who had taken a prize and who had not and where to grab dinner as a group.

"Are you coming, Riley?"

"Actually, I'm very tired. I think James and I are going to go back to the hotel." We weren't the only ones begging off, and soon those of us who had our own plans for the evening began to peel off by ones and twos. James led me to our rental car, which he'd parked after letting me out at the entrance with all my gear, earlier.

"You know," he said, "I would have come around for you."

"And leave me defenseless on some street corner in the dark?"

"You're right," he said, pulling my free arm through one of his, "I wouldn't want to do that to some poor fool of a mugger."

"Nice, dear."

I dozed off on the short drive back to the hotel—it *had* been a long day—but I woke up as James pulled the car into the lot and was smiling at him as he killed the engine. "A nice man would carry my bags up," I tried.

"This nice man has secured certain promises," he said, "about certain bags with...certain smells." My gear bag often smelled like a high school boys' locker room. That didn't stop me from pretending offense when I shouldered it. And my pretend indignation didn't stop him from sidling away from me in the elevator and holding his nose. An elderly couple got on halfway through the ride, and we both smiled politely, him without dropping his hand from his nose, me still in a sweat-sticky T-shirt and sweats. They stood at stiff attention until we got off five floors later.

James and I looked at each other as the elevator doors slid shut behind us, and then burst into giggles. I moved into him, a reaction as automatic as breathing, and he slung an arm over my shoulder, snuggling me close. "You're such a child," I told him.

"Hmm," he responded, and I wondered at his lack of banter for a moment. Then he opened the door and turned me to the right, and I gasped. "You going to take those disgusting clothes off?"

The hotel bathroom glowed in the light of a handful of tea candles and the bath was full, steam rising from the bubbly surface. "How did you—?"

"Called ahead while you were sleeping and offered a fat

tip. I'm lucky you couldn't keep your eyes open, since *someone* wouldn't just let me go get the car alone."

I smiled. "You should know me better," I said, but offhandedly; most of my attention was focused on the steaming water.

Behind me, James tugged my T-shirt up, peeling it away and letting it drop with a damp slap. "Gross," he teased, but he was already tugging at the waistband of my sweats as I reached up to pull the sports bra clear.

I had planned to tease back, but his kiss on the back of my shoulder stopped me cold and I sighed, letting him help me balance as he leaned down and pulled off my shoes, socks, pants, underwear... He turned me in his hands when I was stripped, running the warmth of his palms down my sides over my clammy skin. I shivered, and not from the chill air of the room.

My beaded nipples might have been attributed to the AC, but it didn't matter. James lowered his head, pulling one into his mouth and swirling his tongue around the tip, then giving the other the same teasing treatment. "Salty," he teased, "just the way I like them."

I snorted, but he kissed my reply away—whatever it might have been—and dug hungry fingers into my short waves of hair. Then he pressed me gently back, assisting me into the steaming tub, and made sure I was comfortable. "Book or oblivion?"

"Oblivion," I answered, and he smiled, pressed a kiss to my forehead, and left me to bask.

Sometimes it's good to be pampered.

I tipped my head back and closed my eyes, surrendering to the heat in the water as it soaked my aches away. It had been a long and straining day with five fights before the KO that secured me the gold. The thought of the medal, safely tucked into my bag with my stinky things, made me grin. It hadn't been easy, and some parts had been anything but fun, but now I could relax, at least for a while, and bask in my success. "National Champion," I whispered to the empty room. It seemed like a dream. A fantasy.

I closed my eyes again and sunk deeper into the bath, my mind going once more to that focused, calm place. And with nothing in front of my eyes to study, I drifted into a relaxed doze.

The water was cooling but not cold yet when the bathroom door opened to admit a very naked James. I sat up, my interest piqued, but he only kissed me softly before kneeling beside the tub and producing the loofah he'd had hidden behind his back. He poured my favorite body wash from a travel-sized bottle and the scent of cherry blossoms washed over me as he claimed my limbs one at a time, scrubbing each with loving attention to detail. By the time he started on my neck and back, my entire body was humming with delight. Then he pressed me back, the soapy scrubber traveling a tantalizing path over and around my breasts, and my sigh of pleasure came out tinged with a moan.

"Are we feeling impatient?" he asked. I moaned again, this time not bothering to hide it within a sigh, and his hand went lower, brushing meticulously over each inch of my belly. I held perfectly still, my nails biting into my palms as I struggled to prove my patience, and he finally rewarded me by lowering his hand once again.

The loofah scratched across my clit and through my folds and I arched and cried out, desperate for more sensation as he playfully brought the scrubber away. "Oh, did I hurt you?" he asked.

A trick question. I could still feel the burn of the soap and the scratchy plastic against my sensitive skin, and I wanted more. Much more. I took a shaky breath, ready and willing to beg, but he was feeling generous. He brought the loofah back to my clit, this time pressing down hard as he rubbed, and I moved my hips to meet him. It tingled and burned, the pain translating somewhere between my nerve endings and my brain, transmuting itself into golden delight. The water sloshed as we found our rhythm, my hips bucking and his hand dragging the roughness of the loofah against me over and over.

I was close—so close—my fingers digging into the edge of the tub to give me the leverage to move, when he reached back with his free hand, grabbed a small handful of my wet hair and tugged. The sweet sharpness dropped me over the edge, trembling and crying out. I didn't even realize that I'd gone limp enough to dunk myself beneath the water until I felt James's hand gently lifting me up, steadying me until I could sit up again on my own.

"All clean?" he teased.

It was just then that I realized how cool the water had gotten, and I leaned into his touch, my trembles shifting from those of uncontrollable pleasure to shivers of cold. "Clean," I said. "Happy. Freezing!"

His smile was soft and sweet. "I see that. Come on, champion, let's get you dried off."

He draped my arm around his neck, his half-hard cock bobbing tantalizingly near as he helped me to my feet and out of the tub. He kissed me hard, pressing into me until I barely felt like I could stand on my own two feet, and then stepped back, leaving me weaving as he rubbed briskly with the rough hotel towel.

I stood, eyes closed, enjoying the texture against my sensitive skin and also the warmth that it brought into my limbs after the cool of the water. He dropped kisses across my collarbones and down one arm as he moved down my body, and then knelt before me to dry my legs, his tongue teasing at my navel. I giggled and tried to brush him back, and he captured my hands and bit the tender flesh of my belly in response, drawing something between a screech and a sob out from deep within me.

He'd dried my other leg before I'd gotten my equilibrium back, and I was surprised to see him standing before me, slightly stooped to peer into my eyes. I smiled. "It's that way, is it?"

"Hmm?" I purred. I felt gravity dragging me forward, so I leaned toward him and he caught me by my shoulders.

"Come on, baby, walk this way." He tugged and led me, giddy and pleasantly tingling, toward the bed. "Where do you want it tonight?"

"I pick?" I asked dreamily.

"You pick."

I hummed another purr, considering, and then turned and flopped backward onto the bed. My ass was still half-numb from sitting all day the day before and my legs were tired from the fighting. "Tits," I said, flopping my arms up over my head.

He climbed on top of me, his hands briefly going to my wrists to pin them to the bed. "What's your word?"

I giggled.

"Come on, you know you have to say it."

"Tofu," I said and giggled again.

"That's my girl." He let go of my wrists and stroked my cheeks with gentle hands as he eased back, settling himself more comfortably astride my hips. I felt his cock twitch and settle against my belly, not quite ready to join the fun…yet.

I was so entranced with the sight of it—thickening and darkening and shifting like a living being—that I didn't notice him moving until I felt the sting of a slap against my left breast. I gasped, but the pain wasn't sharp enough to do much more than startle me, and I shifted my shoulders, waggling his targets at him without moving my hands from where he'd pressed them.

His second slap landed on my right breast, and I felt my pussy begin to warm once again. In fact, my whole body was warming, heat pouring through me at the speed of desire.

Two more slaps, one right after the other, came harder, but the stinging pain of the slaps was faint and buzzing inside my head as something greater began to hum within me, floating me away from the pain on a lake of pleasure. I moaned, crying out wordlessly as I stretched myself long, and let the blows, harder and steadier as my flesh warmed from pale to pink to red, rain down.

This was why James had such a hard time with martial arts. For him, hitting was something firmly restricted to the bedroom. And, as his now-impressive erection clearly showed, he also considered that smack of flesh on flesh to be an erotic act.

He paused in the hard slapping, his hands gliding over the outraged flesh with gentleness, and I nearly screamed at the contrasting sensation breaking over me. My whole body felt hot and flushed and my pulse raced. "Please," I whimpered, not having meant to speak at all.

His gentle touches turned rough, fingers digging into the tender, reddened flesh of my breasts. The pleasure shot through me at the bruising grip, and then the sudden change as he lifted his hands away left me dizzy, the room twirling me through a sea of sensations where the input from my eyes felt meaningless. I squeezed them shut, concentrating only on the feelings, my body straining toward his as I awaited the next touch. His hands fell in two sharp blows, one and then the other across my nipples, and then he grabbed them, twisting and tugging mercilessly. Then he held them, pulsing slowly to let gravity add just the right amount of extra tug to my lightly bouncing breasts....

I twisted my wrists to grip the blankets, biting my lip until I tasted blood on my tongue as I sought to stifle the scream. The pain was incredible, shocking through the foggy pleasure that had settled around me, but it knifed straight to my clit, where it was transformed into something else. It was one of James's favorite ways to make me come, and I didn't disappoint him as I let myself slide into the searing pleasure he offered.

He was waiting for me when I was able to catch my breath, hands braced beside my head, hips lifted. As soon as I focused my gaze on his face, he reached down with one hand to line himself up and then *thrust*, stabbing into the wet and heat. I bucked as he filled me, lifting my legs to wrap them around his waist, giving him access to just the right angle to fuck me to the stars.

But he surprised me again, using my grip around his waist to lift and turn me, shifting until we were both more comfortable. And though he was clearly on the edge of excruciating pleasure himself, he slowed his pace, fucking into me with slow, steady strokes that teased and tortured and brought me swiftly to a softer yet more desperate edge.

"You're amazing," he whispered, his voice fringed with rough desire as he pinned me to the bed with his intensity. "My little champion. Show me how you fight for it."

My smile broke through the last of my fog and I gripped his shoulders, hips lifting, body rising as I pressed myself into him, grinding at...just...that...angle...

I cried out loud and long as I fought to *take* my pleasure, and as I won the moment, I brought my biggest supporter along for the ride.

# THE PROPOSAL

Tamsin Flowers

I hate going somewhere when I know I'm going to hear bad news. You know, like the doctor's office for test results when you already know things aren't right, or into class for exam results when you know you screwed up half the questions. Everybody hates those things, right? It was the same feeling I got about going to meet Rick over at Calli's bar a few nights after he got back from his Hawaiian holiday.

Of course, I'd met him there a hundred times before, either with the gang or even once or twice on our own. It was out at the back of the bar I tried to kiss him that one time. It hadn't worked out quite how I wanted—it was a mistake of epic proportions, in fact—and we'd been pussyfooting around each other ever since. Actually, *avoiding* would probably be a better way of putting it. Three years of ducking and diving so we didn't come face-to-face. And, of course, I've been in love with him all that time.

But then he called me unexpectedly and said he had something to tell me. I pretended my calendar was full to bursting but he said it couldn't wait. I knew deep down what it was he needed to tell me. He'd just spent two weeks in tropical paradise with his girlfriend and even before they left, his sister Tanya said she thought he was going to propose. He hadn't been dating the girl long but they were desperately in love, according to more than one source. So, yup, he was going to break the news gently and say how much he hoped we'd still be friends. I would congratulate him and smile, give him a hug and go on my way after assuring him that, of course, we'd still be friends. And perhaps, if I could remember her name for more than a nanosecond, I'd say how pretty his girl was. And inside I'd be slowly dying.

What do you wear for bad news breakage, besides waterproof mascara? Not your best underwear, obviously.

I walked into Calli's and scanned the room. Rick was sitting in one of the booths along the back wall. Good pick, we'd have some privacy if I started to cry. As I made my way across to him I became aware of a tremor in my right arm. I so didn't want to be there. I didn't want to hear about the wedding to which I'd have no intention of going. *Please god, don't let him ask me to be part of the ceremony*, I thought as I reached the back of the bar.

"Lyla," he said, with a smile that evaporated as quickly as it formed.

"Rick," I said cautiously, as I slid into the booth opposite him.

He always looked good, but with a suntan? I had to concentrate on the pattern of his hideous Hawaiian shirt to stop myself openly drooling.

"Like it?" he said.

I looked up, puzzled.

"The shirt. I got it in Waikiki. It's the genuine article."

"It's horrible," I said. "I mean...I'm sorry...I'm just not big on floral for men."

He signaled the waitress and asked for a couple of beers, though he still had a half-finished one on the table in front of him. He caught me looking at it and picked up the glass to finish it off. I noticed that his hand was shaking as he raised his arm.

"Rick, you said on the phone you had something to talk about."

There was no point putting it off any longer.

He put down his glass and licked the foam from his top lip. My heart fluttered in my chest like an angry bird. We looked at each other for what seemed like an eternity.

"You ever been to Hawaii?" he asked.

I shook my head.

"It's nice. I took Teri there because I wanted to propose to her."

Bam! He said it, just like that. I switched on autopilot, ready with my rehearsed lines.

"Congrat—"

He put up a hand to cut me off.

"Wait," he said. "I haven't finished."

He took a sip of the fresh beer. I gulped down a third of mine.

"I booked a table in a fancy French restaurant. We went for cocktails first..."

"Look, Rick, I don't need the details."

His hand came up again to stop me.

"We had dinner and I took her down onto the beach."

I squirmed in my seat.

"There was a full moon, the sea was calm, everything was perfect."

"Stop, Rick..."

"I went down on one knee in the sand and asked Teri if she would do me the honor of becoming my wife. She said..."

I slid to the end of the banquette and started to stand up.

"...No."

I stopped in my tracks. Rick finished his second beer as I sank back down into the booth.

"She said no?" My voice broke to a high-pitched squeak but that didn't matter. Not if she'd said no. I wanted to ask, *Why?* but it wasn't my business. At least she'd said no.

We sat staring at each other and time passed. My breathing sounded labored in my ears. My heart was thundering now—forget birds, this was more like having elephants in my chest—and I still didn't see why Rick had brought me here to tell me this.

Finally he spoke.

"She cried and she said there was nothing more on this earth that she wanted but she had to say no. When I asked her why, she said it was because there was someone else."

"She was two-timing you?"

Rick's blue eyes locked on to mine with new intensity.

"No. It was me. I wasn't two-timing her or anything but she felt totally sure that I had a thing for someone else."

"That's what she said?"

Now I felt stupid. I really didn't get why he was telling me this.

"Yes."

His gaze held me steady and I couldn't look away. A shiver passed through me and I felt goose bumps spring to attention on my arms. I hardly dared allow myself to follow where he seemed to be leading. But finally I did get it and my mouth fell open. Words, however, didn't emerge.

"She was right," he said. "And I hadn't realized it. Not until she pointed it out. She packed her bags and left and I spent the second week sitting on that beach on my own, wondering what I was going to do about it."

Still I couldn't quite believe what I was hearing.

"What...?" I started before my voice failed me.

"That depends on you." His voice quavered.

Our hands met at the center of the table, clutching clumsily, and as we leaned toward each other I knocked over my glass of beer with a clatter. Beer flooded across the flat surface and over the edge into Rick's lap.

"You're going to have to spell it out for me, Rick," I said.

"Not here."

I can't remember the short walk back to Rick's apartment. It wasn't late and the streets were still busy but I think we were pretty much draped around each other in a way that made it quite clear what was going to happen the moment we got behind a closed door.

And it did.

As soon as the door of his apartment swung shut behind us I was able to take my second bite of the apple. That mistimed kiss so many years ago was finally laid to rest as I pushed him back against the wall and offered my face up to his.

"Lyla," he sighed, "I've been so stupid for so long...."

His mouth descended on mine, soft and urgent. My lips were already parted and there was nothing tentative about the way his tongue invaded my mouth. His arms wrapped around my back and pulled me in close against his body and my nostrils were filled with his scent. I felt dizzy—I'd imagined this happening so many times but, of course, the reality was a hundred times more vivid than the longing ever could be. My body was flooded with the sensations of desire and I grabbed a handful of his long blond hair fiercely enough to make him grunt, low in his throat.

Our bodies were pressed tight together, my breasts flattening against the planes of his chest, while lower, against my belly, I could feel the hard outline of his cock. My hips ground against him of their own volition. He put one of his hands up to the back of my head to hold me steady as his kiss became more savage. Our tongues twisted and our teeth clashed against each other. My legs felt weak but Rick had me gripped so firmly that I would have remained in his embrace even if my feet had been lifted off the floor. It was a kiss that seemed to last forever and I was ecstatic with that—as far as I was concerned I never wanted it to end.

But eventually we had to break for breath and as Rick's mouth lifted away from mine I practically sobbed. I still couldn't believe this was happening.

"Come on," he said, taking one of my hands.

He led me to his bedroom and sat me on the edge of the bed. Then he knelt in front of me, resting his forearms on my thighs.

"Wait," he said as I leaned forward to continue our kiss. "Lyla, I just want to say..."

He ran a hand through his hair, seemingly to buy himself some time, and then his face crumpled with pain.

"I know how close I came to fucking this up," he said, "and it scares me. How long would it have taken for me to realize once I was married to Teri? And then what?"

I tucked a hank of blond hair back from his forehead and rested my hand on his.

"But she knew and she did the right thing."

"Thank god," he said, kissing my hand. "But I've wasted so much time fucking about with the wrong girl."

"Girls," I reminded him. Cruel? Maybe—but there'd been several others before Teri came on the scene.

He looked up at me and I saw his blue eyes were brimming with tears.

"I'm sorry," he whispered.

"I was so scared," I said. "I thought you were going to tell me you were getting married to Teri."

I hooked my arm behind his neck to pull him closer and this time his kiss was tender. His mouth played across mine as he softly caressed my jaw with a finger. I pulled on his lower lip with my teeth and he groaned, opening up to give my tongue access. At the same time I started undoing the buttons of his shirt. I needed to see him naked and to touch his skin. I wanted to feel the heat of his body on mine. My hands were shaking and I fumbled. Rick came to my rescue and simply ripped the shirt open, buttons popping off and clickety-clacking on the hardwood floor. My hands went to his chest, feeling the muscle tone under his skin, which was as hot as if he'd just come in from the beach. He shrugged his ruined shirt off over his shoulders and his skin practically hummed under the pads of my fingers as I slid my hands around to his back.

"Oh, Rick," I sighed, as his mouth moved to the hollow at the base of my jaw. There were so many things I needed to say to him but my synapses were only firing on one wavelength and it had nothing to do with talking.

He found the zipper at the top of my dress and as he drew it down my back, a shivery thrill worked its way up me in the opposite direction. Then, as he peeled away the soft jersey bodice, I suddenly remembered the underwear situation. Ropey old bra, a bit gray. Unlucky pants complete with hole.

"Oh fuck!"

Rick froze.

"What?"

"I'm sorry. Please don't look at my underwear. I wasn't expecting this to happen."

Rick laughed and quickly pulled the dress right off me. He sat back on his heels and looked me up and down. Laughing.

"I see what you mean. Not quite Victoria's Secret."

My face burned.

"But you look pretty damn good to me."

There was only one solution. Within seconds I had them off and had kicked the offending articles under Rick's bed.

"Wow!" he said. "Beautiful now."

He stood up and disposed of his jeans just as quickly. He was commando and I had only a second to wonder if he'd anticipated this before he was pushing me back onto the mattress.

Skin to skin at last, our bodies stretched out together and I was enveloped in the warmth and smell of him. I could feel the rough hair on his chest and the slight protrusion of his nipples. His breath was moist on my shoulder and his hands cupped my buttocks so tightly I gasped. His cock pressed into my stomach and I stretched a hand down to it, pushing my way between our torsos. Oh god, I'd waited so long to do this. I'd thought so often about taking him in my hands or in my mouth. And now I could.

I pushed him off me, so he rolled onto his back beside me. My eyes went to the white band across his hips that hadn't tanned in the Hawaii sun. His abs were taut and sculpted, physically perfect, and I reached out to touch his cock. Unrestricted now, it bobbed up and down when I stroked it with my hand. The skin was soft as nappa leather and marbled with indigo veins—but so hard under its delicate covering. I leaned forward and brought my mouth to its tip. His hips bucked up as I brushed my tongue across the apex and he moaned again when I sucked it into my mouth. He smelled wonderful and he tasted even better. I took him in deep and swept my tongue along the underside, feeling the pulse as it grew within my mouth.

I tightened my fingers around its base and started to swirl my tongue and lips up and down the shaft. I could tell it was all Rick could do not to writhe underneath me and his breath sounded increasingly ragged.

"Stop, baby," he said. "You're gonna make me come."

I gave him a nip and turned my head as far as I could to look up at him.

"And I want to be looking in your eyes the first time we're together. Yeah?"

Reluctantly, I relinquished my plaything and worked my way up his body. I sucked one of his nipples into my mouth, leaving a hand on his cock, still working it. His hands stretched down to grasp my breasts, first cupping them and then pinching both nipples between finger and thumb. The jolt of pain fired off a burst of pleasure deep within me and I bit back in reply, making him yelp and then laugh. Oh goodness, there was a lot of potential here.

Rick shifted his hips to lie on his side and I slid off him, so we were both on our sides lying face-to-face. He left one hand on my breast and with the other he went exploring, letting his fingers walk down the ridges of my rib cage, then caress the curve of my belly until I squirmed under his touch. Our mouths met again as he slipped his hand down between my legs. I loved the way he kissed me and the pleasure was magnified by his fingers pushing up into me.

I slumped onto my back and let my legs fall open. Rick followed my lead and rolled over to position himself between my legs.

"I'm so ready for you," I said.

His fingers were still inside me and he slid them in and out slowly as my hips moved in unison with him. His thumb burrowed between my folds to find my clit and pleasure magnified and radiated through me. I gasped.

"I need a condom," he said.

He stretched across to the bedside cabinet and seconds later I was helping him unfurl flesh-colored rubber over his cock. It was all I could do not to grab it with my mouth again but my pussy's need was greater. I lay back on the pillows, drinking in the sight of him kneeling above me with a shy grin on his face and a cock dressed up to party.

Then his body swooped down on mine and I guided him home so he could plunge straight inside me. He was big and a small scream of pleasure escaped my lips as he plowed upward. He paused.

"Okay?" he whispered, his lips brushing the side of my neck.

"Better than okay," I said.

It was all I had wanted for so long. To feel this man inside me, stretching me, to feel the weight of his body bearing down on me and to feel myself pinned underneath. He started moving slowly in and out, grunting as he pressed home and sighing as he withdrew. I pushed my hips up to meet him and he ground against me with small moves from side to side to create friction. Slowly he ramped up the speed, pushing deeper with each thrust, and I wrapped my legs around his waist to give him better access.

The front of his pelvis was now crashing against my clit and I could feel the beginnings of my climax. Rick's mouth on my neck pushed me over the edge and as I spiraled away into another dimension, I heard him whispering the words I'd longed to hear. Then his own orgasm broke with a yell and he pinned me to the bed with a rigid back. I could feel his cock pulsing inside me as my own muscles still throbbed against him. We were both panting, quite literally gasping for air, as he collapsed next to me on the covers.

"Oh, baby," he whispered.

I needed to taste his mouth again, so I gave him a long, gentle kiss.

Later in the dark, as I lay settled in his arms, listening to the rain beating against the window, I realized there was one last thing I needed to ask him.

"Rick, do you still have Teri's number on your cell?"

The arm underneath my shoulders jerked as he half sat up.

"Seriously, Lyla?" he said. "Listen, I promise, I'll delete it first thing in the morning. Okay?"

I grinned at him and shook my head.

"Don't do that. I need to phone her and thank her for making you come to your senses. She must have been quite a girl."

But Rick wasn't interested in discussing Teri. He pulled me back into the circle of his arms and shut me up with a kiss. We both had more exploring to do.

# LOVE LASTS

Kristina Wright

John was the guy of my dreams pretty much from day one. I know, that's not terribly romantic, but there you go. I've never been wishy-washy about what I want once I set my mind on it, and once I set my mind on him, that was that. The great thing is, he's the same way. It was like luck, fate, serendipity brought us together and, once together, we were inseparable. Like that. From first date to wedding date in less than six months. And here we are…

"Is this dumb?" I ask, rather belatedly as we're renewing our vows in less than an hour. "Tell me the truth."

John rests his hands on my shoulders as I look in the vanity mirror, smiling at me while I frown at my hopeless hair. Despite my sister's best efforts, my once-thick hair has been through too much. Radiation, chemo and now this ridiculous humidity have taken their toll.

"No, it isn't dumb. It's romantic and you look sexy as hell, so stop messing with your hair and let's get a move on, woman."

That's John. Matter-of-fact, no-nonsense, shoot-from-the-hip. I know he's not giving me a line of BS because he slaps my ass like he has for the last thirteen years and smiles like he can't wait until we get to fall into that big bed behind us.

"Okay, then," I say, running my fingers through my lackluster curls and taking his arm. "Time to get remarried, babe. Remember, you're stuck with me for life."

His smile doesn't even quiver. "I wouldn't have it any other way. Here's to another thirteen years."

"Or twenty-six."

"Or thirty-nine."

"Fifty-two more years has a nice ring to it."

"Crap," he says, "I can't do the math to go higher, but let's just say 'to infinity and beyond' and get going before they come looking for us."

"They won't. They'll think we're having sex and leave us alone."

He glances at the bed. "Well…"

I poke him in the side, admiring his body in a way I haven't been able to for most of the past year. Yeah, we'll get to that big bed. Soon, soon. I've been waiting for this.

It's a whirlwind, but the best kind of madness. Not as big and fancy as our wedding, but I didn't want that. I wanted the people who loved me most, who had been there for me through our marriage and through this cancer crap, to see us together and happy and beating the odds—in all ways. No one renews their vows at thirteen years, right? But I've never been like other people. The fear of dying— a legitimate enough concern until six months ago, made things like convention and logic irrelevant. The word *remission* led to another word—*renewal*. The renewal of my life, for one, but also the desire to renew my commitment to John. He'd been there through so much, *so much*, I wanted him to know I wasn't going anywhere. I would fight—*we* would fight. And so that's how we ended up renewing our vows in front of my best friend Meghan, who had all the credentials to marry us and had pretty much insisted on flying in from Saint Louis to do it.

I'm still crying happy tears an hour later when we're dancing out on the beach, sand between my toes, the sun just starting to set and casting this photography-perfect glow over all of us, even me with my pasty white skin and the lingering bruises from the last extensive round of blood work. It's perfect, ethereal. I close my eyes and just soak it in, tears slipping from under my eyelids. This, this is what I've been fighting for. This is what I've been living for.

"You okay, babe?" John slips his arms around my waist from the back and gives me a squeeze.

I nod. "Perfect. Right now, I am perfect."

I can feel his erection pressing against my backside. "Yes, you are," he growls and that makes me laugh through the happy tears. He still wants me. God, this man rocks my world so hard.

"We have at least another hour before we can get away," I say, answering the question I know he is going to ask. "But really, I want to leave, too."

"C'mon, lady." He takes me by the hand, his strong fingers lacing with mine in a way that has become poignantly familiar this last year. "I have a plan."

I laugh at his growly tone and follow him down the beach amid the knowing smiles and nods of our friends. The music and laughter continues in our wake, fading beneath the sound of the ocean as we get farther down the beach. John is walking more slowly than I need him to, but old habits die hard. I don't know where we're headed, but after a few more steps, I shriek and take off running—I used to run so fast and I miss it—forcing him to pick up the pace and chase me.

He catches me of course, picking me up off my feet and swinging me around. I slide down his body, as breathless from the hard readiness of him as I am from the short run.

"Where are you taking me?" I ask, though I don't really give a damn. He could take me anywhere and I'd follow.

"Right here." He points up at the lifeguard station, a wood box on stilts. It's empty now, there's no swimming after dark and the sun has slipped from view behind the row of beach houses. He helps me up the weathered ladder and gives my ass a patented smack. "Right now."

"Yeah?" I can't help myself, I'm grinning.

"Yeah," he growls, coming up the ladder behind me. "Just like the old days."

The old days. Back when we were dating and would do it anywhere, anytime. Lifeguard stations, backseats of cars, bleachers at an empty stadium—we were all over each other every chance we got.

"We have a bed, you know," I say, even as I'm hiking up my calf-length dress and shimmying out of my panties.

"We'll get there." He's watching me, not making any move to take off any of his clothing. "But if we're going to renew our vows, I want to renew all of them. Including the part about sex."

"There wasn't a 'sex' part to our vows when we got married," I protest, going after his belt with the same enthusiasm I'd tossed my panties aside. "Love, honor, cherish. There was no 'fuck,' not even a 'make love.'"

"Well there should be."

I don't disagree with him. I'm too busy unzipping his pants and palming his cock. Oh my. Still after all these years, he gets me going. With all my health issues, my libido has been up and down the chart, mostly down, sometimes seemingly dead. But now I know it was only in hibernation because it's back, blessedly so, making me wet enough my thighs are slippery.

"Let me finish that, woman, before you make me pop off in my pants," he says, getting his trousers and underwear down to his knees. "That's as much as I'm taking off. I don't trust those clowns to not come looking for us."

I nod in agreement, watching his erection bob in front of me. "It's, um, enough," I say, suddenly at a loss for words as he fists his cock in his hand. "I can't touch you, but you can touch yourself?"

"I know how much I can take," he grunts, showing me just how he likes it. "And I'm not nearly as excited by my hand as I am by yours."

"I've got more than a hand to offer."

He takes his hand off himself and helps me to my knees. "I'm counting on that."

Sex has been sporadic since the diagnosis, a combination of depression, medication and side effects of the medication. Even since the official "all clear," I've been off my game. But it hasn't just been me—John has had to fight his own demons. Not knowing if, or when, or how hard to touch me, not wanting to put too much on me, physically or emotionally. At times, I appreciated the kid-glove treatment, at other times I resented it. But there's nothing hesitant in the way he touches me now, filling the palms of his hands with my breasts, kneading them through the thin fabric of my dress, tweaking the nipples as they rise to attention.

I moan a little, letting him know this isn't just okay, it's exactly what I need. He pauses, studies my face as if to make sure it was a sound of pleasure and not of pain, and then his eyes get that heavy, lust-filled look I know so well.

"C'mon, babe, I need you," he says, and the words thrill me. He *needs* me. Me.

I let him guide me until I've turned around and I'm facing the ocean, hands braced on the frame of the lifeguard tower. I'm looking out over the ocean, but it's full dark now and I can only hear it, the waves rolling in at high tide. I feel his hands on my hips, then he takes one away. Then I feel him guiding his cock between my thighs, the thick head sliding against the moisture on my thighs.

"Damn, baby," he says, and it's almost a prayer.

I sigh. "I know. God, I need you."

And just like that, he's inside me, fully seated, his forearm wrapped around me, pulling me back against him, holding me steady in the opening to the lifeguard tower. I won't fall, even if my hands slip and I lose my balance. He has me.

"Oh John," I moan, as he moves inside me, finding his rhythm, coaxing me to join him. His cock is hitting that sweet spot inside me and I feel as if I'm blossoming, unfurling from the inside out.

"Yeah, baby, yeah," is all he says, and it's enough, those three words so filled with pent-up passion and frustration, that he's now, finally, able to unleash.

He cups my breast with his free hand, and I'm all that's holding us up, my hands braced on the weathered frame, my nails digging into the sea-salted wood. My knees are protesting the hard platform, but I don't care. I don't care. I've weathered so much more than this little shack, a little pain is only a reminder that I'm still here, I'm still alive, I'm still fighting. I'm still loving.

"Fuck me," I demand, in a voice I barely recognize, even though he already is—fucking me for all he's worth, and that's so, so much. "Fuck me, hard."

He pushes into me deeper and harder than before. His hand leaving my tender breast to brace beside mine on the frame that's creaking with our efforts. We won't fall, we won't. A laugh bubbles up from inside me, a fleeting image of the two of us tumbling headfirst into the sand, breaking both our necks. What a way to go.

"If you're laughing," he whispers in my ear, nipping my earlobe hard enough to make me gasp, "I'm not doing it right." And then he bucks up against me, his hairy thighs pressed against my ass as he gives me everything I asked for, everything I need. "Come, baby. I won't last long. Come for me."

I start to say I don't think I can, I'm not close enough. But then he shifts the arm braced against my stomach and slips his fingers between my thighs, rubbing my clit as his cock drives into me. I feel as if I'll fall without his arm to support me, but I'm not. I'm anchored by my own hands, impaled on his erection, his hand cupping my mound, massaging my clit until I really do feel as if I'm free-falling, spiraling down, down, down with a scream that is lost on the wind and the waves.

"Yes, yes, yes," he groans, an affirmation of my orgasm, an admission of his own. He throbs and pulses inside me, coming, releasing, but holding fast, staying deep.

We stay like that for several long minutes, me looking out into the blank, dark space that is the ocean, the waves rolling on, oblivious to our pleasure.

"I vow to never stop loving you," he whispers in my ear. "I vow to fuck you like this for as long as we can, whenever we can. I vow to fight—with you and for you—until my last breath."

My voice catches in my throat as the tears start fresh. Such happy, happy tears. I can hear our friends in the distance, the music still playing, the celebration still carrying on. We need to get back. To the party, to our lives together, to that big, empty bed that we have for another three nights. "I vow to never give up—on you, on me, on us."

"It's you and me, babe. Forever," he whispers.

I nod in the darkness, my body in remission, my soul refreshed, our love renewed. "Yeah. Forever."

It is a promise. One I intend to keep.

# ABOUT THE AUTHORS

**JILLIAN BOYD** (barenakedlady.wordpress.com) is the author of numerous erotic short stories and has been published by the likes of Cleis Press, House of Erotica and Constable and Robinson. She lives with her adorable boyfriend in London, where she blogs, bakes and dreams about wild, uninhibited romance while hanging the laundry.

**HEIDI CHAMPA** (heidichampa.blogspot.com) has been published in numerous anthologies including *Best Women's Erotica 2010*, *Irresistible, Best Erotic Romance 2012 & 2013* and *Sweet Confessions*. She has also steamed up the pages of *Bust Magazine*.

**MARTHA DAVIS** (facebook.com/quixoticorchid) is an Atlanta-based, sapiosexual writer and devoted reader of erotica, erotic romance and M/M fiction who's made appearances in a wide variety of Cleis Press anthologies. She's currently working on her first novel.

**KIKI DELOVELY** (kikidelovely.wordpress.com) is a kinky, queer, witchy femme who has toured with Body Heat: Femme Porn Tour and whose work has appeared in various publications, including *Twisted: Bondage with an Edge*, *Serving Him: Sexy Stories of Submission*, *Love Burns Bright* and *Bound for Trouble: BDSM Erotica for Women*.

**CLAIRE DE WINTER** is a published novelist and recovering attorney. She lives in the industrial Midwest with her husband and two small children.

**EMERALD's** (TheGreenLightDistrict.org) erotic fiction has been featured in anthologies published by Cleis Press, Mischief and Logical-Lust. She serves as an assistant newsletter editor and Facebook group moderator for Marketing for Romance Writers (MFRW) and is an advocate for sexual freedom and sex-worker rights.

**TAMSIN FLOWERS** (tamsinflowers.com) writes lighthearted erotica, often with a twist in the tale and a sense of fun. Her stories have appeared in numerous anthologies and usually, she's working on at least ten stories at once.

**MALIN JAMES** (malinjames.com) is a writer living near San Francisco. Most recently, her work has appeared in *Best Men's Erotica 2014* and in the best-selling collection, *The Big Book of Orgasms*.

**CRYSTAL JORDAN** (crystaljordan.com) is originally from California, but has lived and worked all over the United States as a university librarian. An award-winning author, Crystal has published contemporary, paranormal, futuristic, and erotic romance with Kensington Aphrodisia, Harlequin Spice Briefs, Ellora's Cave and Samhain Publishing.

**SKYLAR KADE** (skylarkade.com or @skylarkade on Twitter) writes erotic romance, usually of the kinky persuasion. She lives in California and spends her time asking the cabana boys to bring her more mimosas and feed her strawberries while she dreams up her next naughty adventure.

**AXA LEE** (menagegeek.blogspot.com) is an erotica-writing farm girl, who grazes cattle in her yard and herds incorrigible poultry with a cowardly dog. Her partner is finally getting used to answering weird rhetorical questions that begin with the disclaimer, "So this is for a story…" Her work appears in several anthologies.

**ANNABETH LEONG** (annabethleong.blogspot.com) has written for more than thirty anthologies, including *Best Erotic Romance 2014* and *Passion: Erotic Romance for Women*. She is the author of *Get Laid*, an erotic romance about a married couple desperately seeking a place to make love while renovating their home.

**RENEE LUKE** is a multi-published award-winning author, who has written for several houses, but is now self-publishing. She writes stories with rich texture, deep emotions and realist characters. She creates stories where sensual seduces erotic and believes in love, romance and happily-ever-afters.

**SOMMER MARSDEN** (sommermarsden.blogspot.com) is the wine-swigging, wiener-dog-owning, wannabe runner responsible for *Restless Spirit*, *Learning to Drown* and *Angry Sex*. She's written numerous erotic novels ranging from BDSM to zombies and her short work has appeared in over one hundred anthologies and counting.

**TINA SIMMONS** is a tour guide and freelance writer with dozens of credits under various pseudonyms. She lives in the Florida Keys with her partner and a bunch of cats.

**KATHLEEN TUDOR** (KathleenTudor.com) is currently hiding out in the wilds of California with her spouse and their favorite monkey. Her wicked words have broken down the doors to presses like Cleis, Mischief HarperCollins, Xcite and more.

**JADE A. WATERS** (jadeawaters.com) once convinced a boyfriend that the sexiest form of foreplay was reading provocative synonyms from a thesaurus. She's been penning erotic tales in California ever since. Her latest works are included in *Best Women's Erotica 2014* and *The Big Book of Submission*, both from Cleis Press.

# ABOUT THE EDITOR

Described by The Romance Reader as "a budding force to be reckoned with" and as one of the "legendary erotica heavy-hitters" by Violet Blue, **KRISTINA WRIGHT** (kristinawright.com) is an award-winning author and the editor of a over dozen Cleis Press anthologies, including *Fairy Tale Lust* and the *Best Erotic Romance of the Year* series. Her short fiction has appeared in over one hundred anthologies and her nonfiction has appeared in publications as diverse as *USA Today*, *The Good Men Project*, *Good Vibes Magazine* and *Brain, Child Magazine*. She is the author of the groundbreaking cross-genre relationship guide *Bedded Bliss: A Couple's Guide to Lust Ever After* and the HarperCollins erotic romance *Seduce Me Tonight*. She holds degrees in English and humanities from Charleston Southern University and Old Dominion University and has taught English and world mythology at the college level. She lives in Hampton Roads, Virginia with her husband, a lieutenant commander in the Navy, and their two young sons.